Going Home

A STORY OF SURVIVAL

GW00808817

Going Home

A STORY OF SURVIVAL

DORINE V REIHILL

POOLBEG

A Paperback Original
First published 1987 by
Poolbeg Press Ltd.,
Knocksedan House,
Swords, Co. Dublin, Ireland

© Dorine Reihill 1987

ISBN 0 905169 94 8

Cover design by Steven Hope.
Typeset by Busby Typesetting and Design,
Queen Street, Exeter.
Printed by The Guernsey Press Ltd.,
Vale, Guernsey, Channel Islands.

ACKNOWLEDGEMENTS

It would be impossible to name or express adequate gratitude to all the people who have shown me such friendship, generosity and understanding through the years. As I have always said, the last thing I want is pity, but I do need plenty of understanding. This sometimes calls for great patience from those involved in my current life. Without giving them their status for reasons of professional discretion, I would like to name the medical people who looked after me, as well as all those others whose friendship has been invaluable and enduring. I hope that those who may have been inadvertently omitted or whose names I can't remember from the very early days will forgive me and accept that they are not forgotten in my appreciation.

My first appreciation is to all my caring family and in-laws. I would also like to acknowledge the following friends: Dolores Lynch, Demi & Pat Rowan, David & Mo Austin, Jack & Mairin Lynch, Barry & Irene McHugh, David & Deirdre Bolger, Hugh & Pam O'Donnell, Jeff & Ann Smurfit, Michael & Norma Smurfit, Brian & Catherine O'Halloran, Louise Keegan, Nuala O'Gara, Frank Conroy, Denis Murphy, John & Clodagh O'Meara, Charlie & Abbey Hennessy, Tony & Susan O'Reilly, Keith & Daphne Thompson, Peggy Scarry, Bill & Ann Hosford, Ciaran Doyle, Joan Donnelly, Marion Hendron, Liam McGonagle, Margo Tracy, Dot Tubridy, Michael & Gemma Maughan, Avis Maughan, Phyl Keaveney, Fr Dan Breen, Fr J. Deering, Fr Tom Stack, Michael Bradley, Niall McCarthy, Jimmy &

Tanya Stern, Kathleen Harten, Chrissie Branigan, Esther Curran, Bertie Vickers, Elizabeth O'Riordan, Stella McCarthy, Eddie Kells, Marie O'Reilly, the staff of Holy Child Convent, Killiney, and the staff of Tedcastle McCormick Ltd, Head Office.

It would also be impossible to name all the doctors and nurses who have been involved in caring for me since the first days but I would like to acknowledge the following: Mr Gerry Brady, Mr Brendan Prendiville, the late Dr Hugh McCarthy, Mr Michael Chambers, Dr Jim Devlin, Prof John Fielding, Dr Hugh Raftery, Mr Denis Lawlor, the late Dr Tony Keane, Dr Eoin O'Brien, Mr Dan Kelly, Mr Jimmy Sheehan, Dr Niall Gaffney, Mr Vincent Keaveney, Dr Dermot O'Donoghue, Dr Richard Assaff, Dr Denis Liston, Dr Eamonn Kelly, Dr Frank Malone, Dr Ray Hawkins, Dr Michael O'Shaughnessy, Mr Joe Gallagher, Prof Jim Fennelly, Prof M.X. Fitzgerald, Mr Bill Quinlan, Dr Gary Treacy, Mr Brian Regan, Mr John Varian, Dr Brian Maurer, Matron O'Neill, Sister McElligot, Sister Mary Dunne, Sister Francesca, Sister Francis Mary, Sister Baptist, Roseanne Phelan, Teresa Carey, Margaret Hogan, Marie Byrne, Vera Banbury, Mary Kane, Ann Murphy, Kate McAuliffe, Millie Martin, Mary Hoban, Gerry Walker, Mary Gilligan, Joan Hillery, Jenny McEvoy, Mabel Rose, Yvonne Foley, Imelda Sheridan, Sister Gabriel Rohan, Sister Angelis, Veronica Flannery, June Gallagher, Mary Coman, Irene Harrison, Eithne Tarpey, Hilary Sheehan, Jo Nicholson, Mrs Rosaleen and Ann Shanahan, Dermot Foran, Ambulance Crew, Loughlinstown, Waverly Ambulance Staff, Bray Gardai.

I would like to give special thanks to Mary Crotty (Public Relations) for her guidance and patience.

CONTENTS

Introduction   xiii

Part One   3

Part Two   25

Part Three   43

Part Four   57

Part Five   67

Epilogue   81

Index A-Z   85

DEDICATED
WITH ALL MY LOVE
TO FRANK, SHANE AND TANYA
FOR ALL THEIR LOVE

INTRODUCTION

I am immensely privileged to have been asked to write the introduction to *Going Home*, because it is the story of the bravest and most indomitable patient I have ever known in over half a century of medical practice.

I have known Dorine and her family since 1969 when they came to live at Kilcroney. She was a lively, attractive, intelligent young woman with a multiplicity of interests, and, as she says in her story, everything in the world to enable her to have a happy life. No one could have foreseen the ghastly tragedy which was soon to overtake her.

On the morning after her accident a colleague told me what had happened, and I went at once to St Columcille's Hospital to visit her. I was not prepared for what I was to see. The lovely, vital, young woman I had known lay a shattered wreck, with such appalling injuries that it was impossible to believe she could survive. Her question on seeing me, typical of the courage she was to display in a supreme way in the long and agonising years ahead, was, ''Will I be able to hunt this season, Jim?'' Tears were in my eyes and I could hardly answer.

Jim Devlin, MD
Bray, County Wicklow.

IF

If you can keep your head when all about you
   Are losing theirs and blaming it on you,
If you can trust yourself when all men doubt you
   But make allowance for their doubting too;
If you can wait and not be tired by waiting
   Or being lied about, don't deal in lies,
Or being hated, don't give way to hating,
   And yet don't look too good, nor talk too wise:

If you can dream – and not make dreams your master
   If you can think – and not make thoughts your aim
If you can meet with Triumph and Disaster
   And treat those two impostors just the same;
If you can bear to hear the truth you've spoken
   Twisted by knaves to make a trap for fools.
Or watch the things you gave your life to, broken,
   And stoop and build 'em up with worn-out tools:

If you can make one heap of all your winnings
   And risk it on one turn of pitch-and-toss,
And lose, and start again at your beginnings
   And never breathe a word about your loss;
If you can force your heart and nerve and sinew
   To serve your turn long after they are gone,
And so hold on when there is nothing in you
   Except the Will which says to them: 'Hold on!'

If you can talk with crowds and keep your virtue,
   Or walk with Kings – nor lose the common touch,
If neither foes nor loving friends can hurt you,
   If all men count with you, but none too much;
If you can fill the unforgiving minute
   With sixty seconds' worth of distance run,
Yours is the Earth and everything that's in it,
   And – which is more – you'll be a Man, my son!

RUDYARD KIPLING

PART ONE

But trust the happy moments.
What they gave
Makes man less fearful of the certain grave,
And gives his work compassion and new eyes.
The days that make us happy
Make us wise.

JOHN MASEFIELD

The summer of 1976 was one of the last, beautiful, long, hot summers we had in Ireland, what one might call a "normal" summer in Mediterranean terms. It was also the last normal summer of my life. My thirty-three years had been more than good to me. I could even say that by many standards I had led a perfectly happy existence, apart from the intermittent upsets and sadnesses which punctuate everyone's life, and which are a part of life's ongoing experience.

Certainly I had few worries in early September of that year. I had just returned from an extremely memorable business cum holiday trip with my husband, Frank. It was probably the most exciting trip I had ever enjoyed, and it fulfilled a lifelong ambition to visit the Orient.

The journey started in London, where we spent a couple of days before travelling on to Moscow. From there we continued our journey to Tokyo where we joined business associates, a few of whom were close friends which made it all the more enjoyable. Our next destination was Shimonoseki. Some of us travelled there by train, which afforded us an opportunity to glimpse the fascinating oriental scenery during the nine-hour journey. The business side of our schedule included a magnificent banquet at which I delivered a speech in Japanese, much to the astonishment of the male Japanese executives, who had never heard an Irish woman speak in Japanese! I had taken a three-month crash course in that difficult language; my efforts seemed worth while when I received a standing ovation at the end of my speech. I was not so sure of the excellence of my Japanese accent, however, as one of my Irish friends afterwards remarked to me, "Well done, Dorine, I never knew you spoke fluent Irish!" Later she confessed that she certainly didn't! From Shimonoseki we all went in different directions, our business commitments completed. Frank and I travelled to Hong Kong, and from there to Bangkok and finally to Pattaya in the Gulf of Siam for two weeks in the sun. It was the most memorable and enchanting holiday of my life, but having been away for so long from our two children, aged nine and five, we were looking forward to coming home.

We arrived at Dublin Airport after a fourteen-hour air journey on the day when Christopher Ewart-Biggs, the British Ambassador to Ireland, was assassinated. There was an air of gloom and tension which dampened the excitement of our return.

The summer continued with sunshine every day and the temperature averaging 70°. It reminded us of what we now call the "good old summers".

A curious thing happened to me on one of those days. I owned a new convertible sports car and I was driving into Dublin from our home in County Wicklow. I had taken the roof off the car and music was playing on the stereo. As I approached the red traffic lights at Shankill Church I slowed down to a stop. Some people were crossing the road after 12 o'clock Mass at the Church. I saw a little old lady walking on two sticks, carrying a shopping basket. I was overcome by a certain inexplicable sensation as I watched her trying to hurry across the road, obviously fearful of the traffic. Fear, *terrifying* fear, was something I was to learn about in the coming years.

She looked poor, neglected and lonely. I wondered where was "home" for her. Did she have enough to eat? Did anyone who cared ever call to see her? Did she live in a shabby, dark room on her own? I thought of my own life in contrast. My husband and children and happy home, our very comfortable house, the holiday I had just returned from,

4

the coming hunting season. I was filled with a deep sense of foreboding. Why should I enjoy such freedom and health and happiness when there was so much sadness in the world? I turned off the pop music playing on the car stereo and drove off very slowly as the lights changed to green. Some of the sun had gone out of the day. I had a curious premonition. I felt that the good life I enjoyed was shortly going to end. I said a prayer as I passed the church, for the little old lady on two sticks and for myself, for whatever fate lay in store for me. I tried to put the incident out of my mind but it wouldn't go away.

On 19 September my mother-in-law died peacefully in a private nursing home. She had suffered from a stroke seven years earlier and since then had been wheelchair-bound. She was a much-loved, gentle, religious person and it was religion which gave her the will to survive after her husband's death four years previously. Although she never complained of her condition, her sadness was always there. I wrote her obituary appreciation for the *Irish Times* and in it I included the words which she often repeated to me when I visited her: "If only I could walk again . . . ." Little did I know that five weeks later I would be thinking the same thing about myself.

A mellow autumn had arrived and I was settling into my normal routine of running my home, exercising the horses and writing for a few hours each day. I had had two books published in 1969 and 1974, as well as several short stories and numerous articles. That autumn I had started work on a children's fiction story based on two children of different families and religions growing up in a forest area near the North of Ireland border. In fact I had started to walk through the woods of County Wicklow looking for inspiration among the beautiful autumn trees.

When I returned home from hospital in July 1977 all my books of research on the trees and woods of Ireland lay as I had left them on my desk in the study. It is my ambition to accomplish that project some day.

Our daughter Tanya celebrated her sixth birthday on

Thursday 21 October 1976. Kathleen, our devoted house-keeper, and I decided we would have a party on the Friday for her little girl friends. Our son Shane, aged ten since September, decided he would not take part in a girl's party but requested that we keep plenty of the goodies from the tea party for him! They were two lovable, active, happy children. Shane had inherited my love of horses and I was proud to take him out riding with me. I planned to start him hunting at easy local meets that season.

I came from a family of five boys and one girl and most of us were horse-mad in my childhood home. My parents' lives revolved around horses and the main ambition every year was to bring home a first prize from the Royal Dublin Society August Horse Show. Indeed, my father, who died at the untimely age of fifty-four from a heart attack, rarely failed to return without at least one trophy. My mother was equally successful on the show-jumping circuit. But hunting was their first love, as it was for me.

Tanya's birthday party was the usual mixture of tears and laughter, fights and fun and food! After it finished at six o'clock and Shane was happily delving into the leftover goodies for his tea, I went to pack my hunting gear and overnight case in preparation for my friend Ann who was collecting me at half-past six. She drove her own horsebox behind her car as she kept her horses at home and we were to pick up my horse – a beautiful four-year-old-chestnut mare – which I kept in livery at Bill and Fidelma Freeman's stables at Bel Air in Ashford. We were heading for Gorey where we were staying overnight. Our friends, Deirdre and David Bolger, were hosting a dinner party there and stabling our horses for the night. We were hunting the next day with the Shillelagh Hunt at Coolattin and there was to be a "lawn meet" – meaning hospitality dispensed by a generous host whose land we would be hunting over.

Ann and I settled our horses into our friends' stables and went to change at another friend's house where we would be staying the night, and then returned to the dinner party.

The horses were looked after as well as ourselves!

The dinner party was a great success. It contained all the best ingredients for a memorable evening: good company, good food and drink, good music and good humour. It was after four o'clock when we finally returned to our abode for the night. We arranged with our hostess to call us at half-past eight am as the meet was at eleven o'clock and no huntsman waits for people late for hounds. As a child I had been brought up to believe that the eighth deadly sin was to be late for the meet.

I was awakened after what seemed to be only half an hour of sleep, regretting having partaken with such enthusiasm of the hospitality of the previous evening.

"You might as well have a healthy Irish breakfast," our hostess Dolores advised, "it's a wicked day". I could hear monsoon-like rain lashing against the windows and roof. It would have been nice to turn over and go back to sleep for a few more hours, but when you have grown up with five brothers and parents who consider that you are a coward if you don't "take on" a five-bar gate at the age of seven or eight on a 12-hand pony, you don't seriously consider hiding from a few stair-rods of soft rain!

"Your friend Ann said you must be mad and with any luck the meet will be cancelled," Dolores joked as I was already getting my hunting clothes together.

"Then we'd better phone to make sure it's on," I answered. The reply she got from the hunt spokesman was sarcastic in the extreme: "Cancel *what*? It's the Opening Meet! What sort of visitors have you got who are afraid of a few drops of rain? They should stay in their geriatric homes or take up tapestry!" Enough said. We ate our "hearty Irish breakfast" and drove in the torrential rain to the home of our hosts of the previous evening, the Bolgers, who had our horses ready for putting in the horsebox, groomed and shining. By the look of them, they were excited and feeling somewhat better than their owners!

There was time for coffee which the Bolgers had already

prepared for us. "You're mad, the two of you." they said.

"You're right," we agreed, "we are quite mad to those who don't understand what it's all about: *challenge*!"

Our spirits were indeed high as we took off for Coolattin to indulge in what our wiser friends called "so-called enjoyment."

Who, other than a hunting enthusiast, can understand the pulsating excitement of an Opening Meet? We had spent three months getting ourselves and our horses fit. Ann and I arrived in good time, and exchanged greetings with people we had not seen since the end of the previous season's hunting. There is a close camaraderie between hunting people, individuals who might have nothing in common off the hunting field. This probably holds true for all sports, but I always felt it was especially the case in hunting, where courage is brought out in its essence: It is not a question of a lack of fear, but of overcoming fear. Certainly, if you earn the name of being cowardly on the hunting field you do not rate very highly in anyone's estimation. In the sport of hunting one shares the ups and downs (literally, as well!), being aware of qualities of horsemanship and courage and helping others in trouble — sometimes at the risk of missing a "good run". It involves the whole business of survival: coping with horses, fences, the elements and the unknown territory where the fox and hounds lead you. The pageantry itself is infectious. I realise that anyone who is engaged in anti-blood sports campaigning has probably thrown down this story in disgust at this point. However, I have a confession to make — one which would make my ancestors (most of them masters or huntsmen of hounds) turn in their graves — and that is that I am always secretly delighted when the fox eludes the hunt, especially after a good run.

So much for my defence of hunting! At half-past eleven on that fateful Saturday morning about forty of us trotted off behind the Master and huntsman, all happily agreeing that we *were* quite mad but that we would not change places for anything on that morning in October.

8

"I'm afraid we're going to have to rely on our personalities at the after-hunt drinks," I remarked, looking around at our friends' hairdos rapidly becoming undone and make-up streaming down their faces as a result of the rain. "The looks have had it!" Little did I realise what I would look like ten hours later.

The first draw was a blank. We jumped a few fences to head for the second covert which warmed our blood and enthusiasm. We got a short run from the second draw where a few first-time fallers of the season gallantly slushed their way through mud to recapture their steeds.

One Irish journalist, Kevin Myers, writing about the story of my survival gave this account of foxhunting folk:

But the truth is that certain things happen to certain people because they can take them. Your fox-hunting fraternity, for example, are born to toughness. They can drink a rugby club under the table, go to bed at half past six, get up twenty minutes later to go to hounds, spend the day tally-hoing about the countryside and jumping stone walls that I would not try to go over in anything less than an airliner. They fall off, they bounce, horses roll on them and just as they get to their feet another wave of horses sweeps over the wall and they are knocked arse over tip all over again. But does this stop them? Not a bit. They sprint after their horse which has only galloped on three or four miles after the fall, mount it and set off again in pursuit of the fox.

Next we were cantering along the country byroads in the pouring rain to a third covert where we galloped around in pursuit of the hounds, who I suspect had the sense to try and keep warm rather than go in pursuit of a fox.

At around three o'clock the Master decided to call it a day. Nobody objected, since the season was now well under way. There was a winter of "glorious uncertainty" ahead.

We all went about the practical business of unsaddling our

drenched horses, rubbing them down to dry them off and putting them safely in the horsebox with fresh hay and water. Their warm mash would come later when they were returned to their stables.

We drove to Gorey where we had arranged to meet some friends in French's pub. One of the most cosmopolitan pubs in the country, it is run by John French, one of the best-informed people in Ireland, and his charming wife, Una. No self-respecting person could pass by French's on a journey to *anywhere*! Like the *News of the World*, all human life is there, in fact it transmits the news of the world. From the stock exchange to scandals, computers to charities, Zionism to zoology, you'll always find someone there to discuss your pet subject.

We met our friends as arranged. The Bolgers still thought we were mad, with hair and make-up dripping, and looking very smug at our achievement in having braved the elements, before braving the eloquence of the cognoscenti of French's.

Ann and I ordered soup and sandwiches and hot whiskies. Someone suggested that we should change from our drenched hunting clothes to dry slacks and sweaters. But we were anxious to get the horses home: it was a thirty-nine-mile drive to Bel Air. So we just exchanged our sodden hunting coats for hacking jackets. If I had changed out of my knee-length leather hunting boots, I would undoubtedly have lost both my legs.

We finished our lively chat and thanked our friends for all their hospitality with a cheery "See you next week!". How presumptuous can one be? I thought afterwards. Now, whenever I hear people say, "See you next month, next year", or whatever, I always think of how little we know of what lies ahead.

Our first stop was Bel Air stables where the staff had already left out a covered, warm evening mash for my beloved mare, Siobhán. She had dried out, so we put on her night rug and gave her the mash. She snuggled up to me — more out of comfort than gratitude I suspected — and I said,

"Goodnight, old girl, see you Monday". I never saw her again; I sold her from my hospital bed after months of trying to resign myself to the fact that I would not be hunting again for a year or two!

We drove on to the Willow Grove Pub where I had arranged to meet my husband, who had been golfing, and some friends who had been on a "hunting ride" at Bel Air in preparation for the Bray Harriers Opening Meet the following Saturday. Ann was going on to a dinner engagement so she pulled her car up outside the pub while I ran in to ask one of my friends to give me a hand to move my hunting saddlery and overnight clothes into his car, in case my husband was late. At this hour it was still lashing rain and very dark. Leaving my handbag in the pub, my friend Bill and I went out to remove my gear. The music was still playing on the car stereo as we untangled our two saddles from the rear seat. Bill took my case and left it on the driver's side of the car, while he carried my saddle and wet hunting jacket to his car some twenty yards away, saying he would come back to give me a hand with the other bits and pieces. There still remained the usual female paraphernalia of make-up bag and other items, as well as my hunting crop, gloves, stick, etc. which I had to take out of the boot of the car. I spoke to Ann through the passenger door before closing it and going to the boot.

I vividly recall standing there with my finger on the button to open it when I received a blow to my back. I also remember shouting, *"My God, what's happening?"* The car began to draw away. I had been thrown by the force of the blow from the horsebox onto the boot of the car and I felt myself slipping down onto the towbar. I screamed, "Help, Ann, STOP, Bill! I'm caught on the towbar!" I heard no human voice as the car moved away, gathering speed while I clung to the towbar, screaming hysterically. It was an elaborate towbar with many safety attachments, which ironically probably saved my life, as I was tossed around against the road from every angle, holding onto everything

11

I could hold and screaming all the time. I could hear my own high-pitched voice shouting H . . . E . . . L . . . P Apart from the sound of the music from the car stereo and the lashing rain there was no sound until a few hundred yards up the road I heard a dog barking frantically.

I realised with horror at this stage that I was in a life or death situation. The chances of surviving if my friend didn't hear me were slim. I felt I was going to die but I was determined to do everything I could to survive. My first idea of escape was to jump from the towbar onto the side of the road. But the instinct of human survival is extraordinary. I think it possibly transcends one's normal intelligence in times of great challenge and that hitherto untapped resources give one the strength to think rapidly and with inspiration never before called upon. Every thought was churning in my mind while I was tossed and turned as if in a liquidiser on the freshly tarmacadammed road, the rain lashing around me. I had made a quick decision about throwing myself onto the roadside. Some sixth sense told me that there was a great risk that I would not clear the wheels of the horsebox which was wider than the car and consequently I was in danger of having my back or head or neck run over. I decided to cling on. I knew that there was a YIELD or STOP sign at the end of the lane which led onto the main Dublin-Wexford dual carriageway. It was only a few yards as far as I could remember. If Ann slowed down or stopped there was a good chance I could throw myself clear of the horse-box with safety. What I did not realise was that the distance between the Willow Grove Pub and the end of the lane was nine-tenths of a mile! (police measurements the following day). Neither was I aware, due to my determination to survive, of the horrific injuries which were being inflicted on me as I churned around on the towbar that black, rainsodden October night. Kevin Myers gives a graphic description of this terrifying experience which leaves little to the imagination; but what happened is almost beyond imagination and the horror of that journey is always with me, in some

12

ways dictating everything I do either mentally or physically. I quote him, because during the actual journey I was never aware of pain or the injuries which were mounting in seriousness.

"I never lost consciousness for a minute," Dorine remembers. And her memory of that drive for almost a mile is perfect as she was trailed in the wake of the car, bouncing along the road and clinging, clinging so that the damned horsebox would not claim her, and the injuries began to accumulate. *Her legs broke. So did her arms. And her wrists. One of her hands was smashed. Her skull was shattered. Several vertebrae in her back had cracked.* (*Irish Times,* August 1985)

After what seemed an eternity I was aware of the car engine slowing down. I prayed with what might have been my last words that the sign was a STOP and not a YIELD sign – and if it was a YIELD that there would be some traffic coming up the dual carriageway so that Ann would have to stop. Ann happened to be a very good driver, having spent some years rally driving. She was also a "natural" at driving a horsebox – something I was always terrified to do myself!

Mercifully the car pulled to a stop. I didn't know what position I was in or the extent of my injuries. All I know is that I was determined to get off that towbar as fast as possible! To this day no doctor can understand how I possibly survived what I attempted. I was still screaming to my friend as I threw myself three feet clear of the horsebox.

It may have been some hallucination, but I believe the last thing I heard as my friend drove off (still not hearing me) was Frank Sinatra singing, "I Did it My Way". Certainly it was not the way I would have chosen to do anything! I heard her car and horsebox drive off in the distance. I was aware that I was on the side of the road facing the dual carriageway, only a foot or two away from a county council ditch. A deep ditch. I knew that if I fell into it I had no chance of survival. It was not a night when anyone would be out walking. "I must move out of the way," I thought. I made an effort to stand up. My arms wouldn't work. Even more alarming was the stark and horrible realisation that my legs wouldn't move. I remember vividly shouting out again, "My God, my LEGS are broken." I did not try to move any more. I lay there wondering if there was any further hope of help. I could feel the sticky, thick feeling of blood on my face mingling with the rain which was still lashing down in the black dark night.

Part of me was numb, part of me was in agony, but most of all I was worried about the one thing since the horsebox had hit my back and broken several vertebrae: SURVIVAL. What if a car should drive up the lane (it was one-way)? The chances were it would run over me. What if a blood-thirsty dog came along? I was blinded with rain and bleeding head injuries and presumed I was a pretty bloody sight. My hacking jacket had been ripped off on the journey. It was found in bits and pieces along the road from the pub. My glasses were found where the horsebox had hit me outside the pub. Futile plans went through my mind about crawling to the pub. To show the futility of these plans, here is the report of the first doctor who arrived on the scene one hour after the accident.

I was called to a Road Traffic Accident at approximately 9 pm. I went immediately to the scene of the accident where I found a woman lying on the road. She was very seriously injured and in a very critical condition. The Gardai were at the scene when I arrived. It was a very dark, cold and wet night.

The woman, who I was informed was a Mrs Reihill, was partially covered with a man's coat. She was conscious, in a distressed state and obviously in very great pain. She was also clinically shocked. I removed the coat to observe the extent of her injuries. She had a severe injury to her left temple area with what looked like brain tissue protruding from a fractured skull.

She had a compound fracture of her left femur. The femur shaft was visible and actually lying on the road. The lower end of her left leg (from the fracture distally) was bent backwards so that she was actually lying on it. She had other widespread lacerations and injuries too numerous to mention. I could feel a fast and weak pulse in her left radial artery. I spoke to her and tried to reassure her until the ambulance arrived. I tried to put an intravenous drip in her right and left arms but was unable to do so due to her shocked condition. I helped to get her into the ambulance with the help of the ambulance crew. I accompanied her to St Columcille's Hospital where her case was taken over by the hospital doctors.

I write this, not for any morbid reasons, but to show the extraordinary challenge the team at Loughlinstown Hospital faced during the next twenty-four hours and how enormous was the fight for survival facing me and the medical team in charge of me during the following year.

It was approximately quarter past eight now on the roadside. After what may have been two or five or ten minutes I heard the sound of an approaching car on the lane. I was aware all the time of the sounds of passing vehicles on the dual carriageway, all too far away for rescue. I heard a car pull up, close to me, a car door opening, and the horrified shrieks of children. Then the sound of a kind human voice caused me to feel near elation. I was aware of a lady speaking to me and I tried to tell her exactly what had happened and that my friends were down the road in the Willow Grove Pub. I asked her to go down and tell them of my accident. I didn't realise that the poor woman at first sight didn't know if I was an injured human or animal!

The first thing she did was to comfort her three or four young children in the car, and then she stoically walked over to the edge of the dual carriageway, hoping to stop the first car that passed. Unfortunately, but understandably, drivers are not inclined to stop these days for people out on their own on a wild winter's night, and several cars passed without stopping.

Eventually a kind lorry driver realised she was in distress and pulled up. She explained the problem to him and I heard them both talking about what they should do. I repeated that a lot of my friends were down in the pub and that if they only knew what had happened they would take care of the situation.

I am not sure which of them stayed with me but within minutes my friends had arrived. It was all like a dramatic movie. Dramatic it was, movie, unfortunately, it wasn't!

My friends seemed to carry out their assigned roles with military discipline. Some went back to the pub to phone in turn for an ambulance, doctor, priest, police, my husband and family. Two of my men friends propped me up to stop me swallowing blood and choking. Two of the women who were my best friends in the hunt asked me to try and describe what had happened. One tried to hold my hand but I screamed with pain. My two arms were broken, both at the elbows and the left was broken at the wrist as well as two fingers. Both my legs were inside out.

Meanwhile, the friends who had gone back to the pub were having great difficulty in locating a doctor on duty. They had a quick response from the police and the Loughlinstown Ambulance Service but unfortunately the ambulance driver was given the wrong address and had gone to Delgany, therefore by-passing the spot where we were. It was only after calling eight or nine doctors that they eventually got through to one who had just come in from a call.

During all this time my friends were trying to comfort me and I kept asking for my husband. I knew I was dying and I wanted to say goodbye. Two of my men friends had gallantly taken it in turns to remove their jackets to put around my shoulders as they propped me up. There used to be a joke among us in the hunt that one of the men was a terrible bore after a few drinks and we used to tease him about this. It was all in good fun, and in fact he was really well liked and a complete gentleman.

At one stage one of my friends asked me, "Do you know who has his coat around you and is holding you up?"

"No," I muttered.

"Charlie C!" she said.

"Oh my God," I remember saying (and so does everyone else including Charlie) "wouldn't it be just my luck to die in the arms of the greatest bore in Dublin!"

It was now over an hour since I had been found on the side of the road. There were two police patrol cars, the doctor had arrived and several friends as well. They were still trying to contact my husband. Some people couldn't bear to look at me as apparently I resembled a bloodied rag doll, with my head a mass of exposed tissue and my leg, according to one friend, "inside out like a broken, discarded rag doll." I was not, I imagine, a pretty sight. Thankfully I had no idea at this time of what I looked like or the extent of my injuries but I guessed I was a pretty serious case. Someone had contacted my friend Ann who had been driving the car and she was obviously in as deep a state of shock mentally as I was. It was only when two kindly guards arrived at her house to see the horsebox that she realised the horrific nature of the accident which had taken place. It must have been impossible to believe that only twenty-four hours earlier we were enjoying the best of health and fun with Gorey hospitality.

Shock is hardly an adequate word to describe her reaction. To think it should happen to the two of us who for several years had hunted together, sharing the same challenges and competition, and scheming at times to get a day off for a Sunday hunt!

She was already on her way to St Columcille's Hospital in Loughlinstown before I arrived there. The ambulance eventually, through police radio communication, located us. Everything was grim and business-like – friends scattered under instructions. The doctor tried to console me as I let out a scream of agony when the ambulance men expertly tried to "unfold" my legs — or what was left of them. I begged for one of my friends to be allowed to stay with me in the ambulance on the way to the hospital and was assured that that was no problem. Then I saw her being pushed back as they closed the ambulance door with the words, "Sorry, Miss, we need all the space we have." It was not one particular aspect of the accident which amazed every doctor, it was that I never lost consciousness and was acutely aware at each moment of everything that was said or happened.

I had asked to be taken to St Vincent's Hospital where I knew some of the doctors. I was assured that this was no problem. Of course I had no idea what hospital I was being brought to as we arrived after a very fast journey with ambulance sirens wailing. It was St Columcille's in Loughlinstown, some six miles from the scene of the accident.

The ambulance men rapidly pulled up at the front door and rushed to the back to put me on a stretcher and carry me into the hospital. I heard voices.

"Get out of the bloody way, this woman is *dying!* " said an irate ambulance-man. I thought I recognised the voice of the person in their way.

"Is it Mrs Reihill?"

"Yes, it is, now get out of the way."

"It's my wife," I heard my husband say.

"Sorry, sir," muttered the ambulanceman, "we must get her to theatre. Stay with us if you like."

My poor husband, who couldn't bear the sight of a pin-prick or a child's cut finger without almost fainting! What a ghastly scene it must have been. Doctors and nurses arrived as I was wheeled along the corridors to be "prepared" for theatre. They did not have to worry too much about taking off my clothes. They were already in shreds. My new leather knee-high hunting boots had without doubt saved my legs from being amputated on the roadway, whatever about immediate worries about future amputation. But that Saturday night they were all only interested in my surviving the night. As we were joined by nurses and doctors on the way to the theatre, I asked a doctor, "Are *both* my legs, broken?"

His reply left little room for doubt. "Are they *what*?" he replied in a typical Irish fashion – where a difficult question is always answered with another question!

Sister Angelis, the Matron, was in charge and endeavouring, magnificently, to cope with the crisis. They efficiently went about the professional business of getting me to theatre to start work as quickly as possible. One learned and experienced doctor who was used to traffic accidents told me a year later that I was the most awesome and awful mass of injuries he had ever seen.

Meanwhile family and friends were gathering as word spread of the horrific accident. I was aware of their presence but was oddly elated myself, in contrast to the grim and green-faced visitors who came to see me. I talked non-stop and was quite high, trying to calm down the more worried-looking members of family and friends, with trite jokes about "not being able to kill a good thing" and "can't get rid of a bad penny". If I had known what I looked like I might have given up through sheer vanity! Although it had been a wet and muddy hunt, I doubt if there was any comparison between the bedraggled rider of the early morning and the horrifyingly bloodied and disfigured body on the stretcher. I'm sure an odd fox in the country would have had a wry smile at my condition.

I cannot praise sufficiently the staff at St Columcille's Hospital. They calmed and comforted me, clarified problems, and went about their business with admirable professional and medical efficiency.

I think I was in the room beside the theatre before being brought in for "whatever we can do", as I overheard one doctor say to a distressed member of my family. In another area I could hear two other people discussing (or arguing, really) with a nun whether I should have the Last Rites.

"There's a priest here in a room nearby," the nun said.

"Is she that bad?" asked my husband. "It might frighten

her."

"I think she should have the choice herself," said someone else. At this point I burst out to a nurse: "Oh for heaven's sake, if there's a priest around I'll take whatever's going." And the priest arrived immediately – I firmly believe he was waiting next door! – and performed the Last Rites in a wonderfully gentle and sensitive manner. I was asked if there were any persons in particular I wished to see (one at a time) before I was brought to theatre and I asked for a few of the people closest to me. Many were drenched and muddy from the roadside "vigil", many were green in the face at what they saw, and some were speechless. I tried to talk and joke my way through. I was told afterwards that when one talks so much in shock and after losing so much blood one is usually very close to death.

In theatre they set to work with caring efficiency.

"We'll have to cut off your hunting boots, I'm afraid," a masked surgeon explained gently. "Your legs are too injured to pull them off." I made a painful effort to sit up with no success and settled for what I hoped was a threatening look – can you look threatening with a fractured skull and a head full of tarmac and blood? Frightening, perhaps, but not threatening.

"Hey, they're *new,* and *real* leather!" I protested weakly, "I'll sue you for these." They proceeded to cut off the remains of my hunting breeches and undergarments. "Are you frightened?" a nurse asked gently as she held one of my bloodied hands.

"Certainly not! Hunting people don't get *frightened,"* I said with what I hoped was a certain measure of disdain. I gave up the unequal battle to save my dignity and was soon mercifully put out of my agony with an anaesthetic. Just before the anaesthetic, I was thinking of the advice the mothers of my generation gave us: "Always wear clean underwear *every* day, dear, you never know when an accident might happen away from home." A funny thought to die with, come to think of it. Maybe the Lord decided to preserve

me for more fitting thoughts for my demise.

I learnt later that most of my family and friends waited till around three o'clock in the morning, when they were advised to go home as the doctors were still "doing their best".

Most of them went back to my home which was about five miles away, where they stayed up all night, phoning the hospital every half hour or so. At six o'clock my husband received a phone call from one of the surgeons in theatre, telling him that they had done their best and I had come through "reasonably well – considering . . ."

"You mean the operation was a success?"

"I'm sorry, Mr Reihill, your wife is nowhere near operation stage. We have just spent the last seven hours trying to remove as much tarmac and dirt as possible from her wounds. I think you should all get some sleep for a few hours."

PART TWO

To prove
Our almost - instinct almost true,
What will survive of us is love.

PHILIP LARKIN

I regained conciousness at around half past eight on Sunday morning. A gentle, smiling nurse was standing looking at me. I was totally confused and in great pain. I tried to move but none of my limbs would respond. I asked the nurse what had happened and realised in panic, as she bent close to me to hear what I was trying to say, that my voice had gone.

Realising my panic, she explained gently that I had been in a serious accident and that my voice was temporarily lost through shock. I noticed on her uniform badge that her name was Sister Gabriel Rohan – Rohan was my own maiden name. She asked if I would like some water. I nodded and my head felt as if it was smashed in a hundred pieces. She gave me a few sips of water from a teaspoon.

I lay there trying to recall events of the night before – the horsebox, the towbar, my friends around me in the dark rain, the ambulance, Frank – but it was too much effort to make sense of it all in my befuddled brain, or what was left of it. I didn't know if I was falling in and out of sleep or in and out of consciousness. The next thing I heard was the familiar voice of my friend Louise Keegan who had been holding my hand on the roadside the previous night. I heard her requesting to see me and Sister Gabriel replying: "I'm afraid not, she's very seriously injured and is only allowed to see her husband."

"But she will probably ask if I called," Louise said. I tried to make signs to Sister Gabriel to allow her in but she had her back to me. In frustration I tried to speak. "That's my friend, please let her in," I tried to say, but my voice wouldn't work. With frustration and misery I heard my friend telling the nurse to let me know that she had called. The next voice I heard was also, happily, a familiar one. It was my family doctor and close friend, Dr Jim Devlin, who had just received news of my accident and had come immediately to the hospital. Sister Gabriel was also refusing admission to him but to my delight his much loved familiar voice insisted: "But I'm her family doctor, of course I can see her" and in he came. I made a supreme effort to put on a cheerful face, not realising what a mess I looked. In his professional way he displayed no shock but leaned over the bed in an attempt to catch my weak whisper. His eyes visibly filled up momentarily as he realised what I was trying to say. He recalls now with a smile (ten years later) that what I was saying was, "Will I be able to hunt again this season?"

"Of course you will, my dear, knowing you!" he reassured me. He admitted some years later that he did not think I would live through that day.

I do not remember any more of that day but afterwards learnt of the frantic efforts of my family to find out from doctors in charge of my case the extent of my various, very serious, injuries. I had a fractured skull and both my legs were broken; my right knee was "a hole just full of dirt and tarmacadam," while the soft tissue of my left leg was almost totally eroded and my left hip was almost non-existent. Both arms were broken at the elbow and my left wrist and several fingers were broken. In addition there were other lesser injuries, broken vertebrae in my back, and numerous bruises, lacerations and cuts, so that I was almost unrecognisable.

Because of the extent of my injuries, my family wanted the best surgeon in each field to be immediately available if I survived the first couple of days. They even called contacts abroad for advice on the experts in each medical field. They were told "You have the best in Ireland", which was at least some comforting reassurance they could grasp onto. The fact that I am today walking with a stick and able to write this story bears out the high esteem and confidence in which the Irish medical profession are held world-wide.

The next few weeks and even months went by in a haze. The odd hour of lucidity. A vague awareness of being surrounded by strangers and sometimes of visits from my brother or husband. I was changed from one hospital to another, depending on the urgency of attention to various injuries. I had nurses "round the clock". Death was never far away in those first months.

My first move from St Colmcille's was to Jervis Street Hospital by ambulance on the Tuesday following my accident when they decided that since I had survived the first traumatic twenty-four hours it was time to consider how to start "putting me back together again." At Jervis Street Hospital the renowned Mr B took over. I remained there for a few days, between life and death, while my future surgery was being assessed. I was then moved to Dr Steevens' Hospital where the senior plastic surgeon in Dublin, Mr P, was to take over the immediate surgery in association with Mr B.

I remember the agony of being carried on the stretcher to a room in Dr Steevens' Hospital where I was met by a lovely young nurse from Mrs Shanahan's Nursing Agency. I must pay tribute here to Mrs Shanahan for her extra- ordinary instinct for "matching" nurses with patients, carefully considering each case in question. I am eternally grateful to her for making sure I was taken care of by a constant stream of skilful and cheerful nurses during the two years when I needed nurses around the clock. In fact I can recall only one instant of insensitivity by a nurse in the ten years since my accident, and in this case I had interviewed the nurse myself! It was the time when I was extremely ill and in great pain with a pulmonary embolism (a clot on the lung). It was at the end of the nurse's shift one day, when another nurse would take over around three o'clock in the afternoon. She said she had forgotten her make-up and asked if she could use mine. At this time I had no part of my face on which I could put make-up myself but someone had brought in my make-up case and it lay in the bedside locker. I said "Certainly, help yourself."

She took out the bag and sat in front of a mirror doing up her pretty face. Suddenly I was seized with agonising pain in my lung. "Nurse, please," I gasped. "I'm in agony: please can you get me something for pain?" Without even turning to look at me she said impatiently, "Oh for heaven's sake, with your injuries what do you *expect?*" To my amazement and horror she carefully continued to apply make-up. I swear if my prayers were answered that moment, she would have had a rash on her pretty face that would make a leper look unmarked by comparison. Tears streamed down my face while she calmly left the room. One of my favourite nurses came on duty a few minutes later. She rushed to relieve my pain and distress. I never saw the other nurse again.

On the subject of prayer, so many people have said to me things like, "You must have had great faith in prayer," or "You must have received great consolation from your faith." Well it wasn't quite as straightforward as that. I have always been a religious person but very much in a questioning way. Certainly I believe there is a God, but I don't understand His ways except through Christ and the Blessed Virgin and my "favourite" saints. But I have always found it difficult to adore and worship *God* himself, because I find it hard to relate to him, being only human myself. I find it easy to relate to Christ and to His mother and the saints even though I never met them, because I can love them as fellow humans. I would explain this *love* of people one has never met by pointing out the simple fact that people can love each other who have never met but who have maintained constant communication, as in the case of pen pals.

Following my accident I was inundated with every sort of religious aid, receiving hundreds of Mass cards, letters offering prayers, Novenas, Mass bouquets and so many relics that I could have made a holy patchwork quilt. In addition, there were visits from various priests, either friends or well-meaning strangers. Depending on how ill I was, I received these kindnesses in an attitude varying from great hope to total indifference. It was a source of regret to me that in the early days I could not receive Holy Communion, due to the fact that I was vomiting so frequently.

There were also one or two humorous incidents which I recall. A friend of mine had as a very close friend a priest who was devoted to a certain saint. When he heard of my story and the fact that I was so close to death, he considered it an ideal opportunity to show his faith in the saint and his power to produce a miracle.

He was, I heard later, caught up in his own enthusiasm to the point of exhilaration, thinking of the glories that lay in store should he succeed in his "mission".

One afternoon, he arrived uninvited and unannounced, so when the nurse asked if I would see Fr X I presumed it was the hospital chaplain and I said, "Certainly".

Fr X entered the room and I greeted him as cheerfully as I could. He was very pleasant in his introduction. He told me that he had heard of my accident through a mutual friend, and had decided to come to see me, as apparently he considered me ideal "miracle material".

Without further words he then proceeded to perform an extraordinary little ritual, which stuck me in my speechless state as a performance coming somewhere between that of a witch doctor and Paul Daniels.

He knelt down, got up, mumbled some prayers, blessed me, shook Holy Water everywhere and did a sort of little dance around the room with what looked like an old duster but which he said was a holy relic. He was tiny in stature – about five feet tall – which made his performance all the more leprechaun-like. When he had finished he came close to the bed again and said with great faith and total confidence, "I know you're going to be fully cured, Dorine, you are *ripe,* I repeat, *ripe,* for a miracle!"

I felt quite irreverent in having such an amused reaction but he really was quite extraordinary. Also, I had felt such a sense of hopelessness with my own unanswered prayers, that I hoped Fr X might have more success with his somewhat unorthodox performance. I gave him a Mass donation and thanked him for his visit.

The next day he arrived again and I witnessed the same ritual. This went on every day for the next week or so until I felt that maybe others would benefit more from his enthusiasm. I also felt that he had given me enough of his time already. The novelty was beginning to wear off.

On what must have been his tenth visit, I thanked him as profusely as possible for his kindness and concern. I decided to tell him that I was going home on the following day. ("Oh what a tangled web we weave, when first we practise to deceive. . . .")

His immediate reaction to my deception was to jump up and down with sheer ecstasy , shouting "A miracle! A miracle! Oh *Thank you* God!" Followed by: "Well done, St X!" He left in high delight. I never saw him again and quietly asked the nurses to read out the obituary columns for a day or two as I half expected to come across the demise of Fr X, "suddenly, after visiting Jervis Street Hospital . . ."

A few days later it was planned to move me to another room, more cheerful and cosy. I was expecting my husband's daily lunch-time visit when at midday two hospital porters arrived to lift the rotary bed (with me in it) to the room next door. They successfully manoeuvred it out of the narrow door after some difficulty and carried me to outside the door of Room 2 where they encountered a major problem.

"It won't fit," said one of the porters.

"It must fit, the doors are all the same size."

They pushed and pulled at different angles till I thought I would be sea-sick.

Two nurses arrived to offer to help to keep me calm. They all tried pushing it in backwards and forwards without success.

"Lift it higher and turn it sideways," suggested a bright nurse. I objected strongly.

"We'll have to put it down on the floor and send for Sister," they finally decided. And so I was unceremoniously lowered on to the floor in front of the main desk till Sister arrived.

Passing patients and visitors looked at me curiously, and with evil glee I closed my eyes and pretended to be a corpse, till I heard one lady exclaiming hysterically, "Merciful Jesus, she's dead! Lord have mercy on her."

Sister arrived full of authority and optimism.

"I'm sorry about this, Dorine, what on earth's going on?" The two nurses and the porters all tried to answer at once:

"The bed is too big."

"The door is too narrow."

"We'll have to put her in another room."

"Nonsense, of course it will fit," said Sister. "Anyway all the other rooms are full. Come on, let's try again." And up they hoisted me again with Sister organising and navigating with all the skill and authority of a naval commander. But eventually she, too, had to admit failure.

"There's only one thing for it, then. The door will have to come off. Put her back on the floor. You don't mind, do you Dorine? I'm sorry about all this."

I said I didn't mind at all, except that I was shortly expecting a visit from my husband and one of my surgeons.

"Well, quick, run for the tool box Mick." "Please, Jesus," I heard her mutter, "Let's have her installed before her husband and Mr B arrive." I presumed it was a prayer.

Mick returned and after more discussions, arguments, suggestions and some "woodwork" the door was finally removed and I was ceremoniously installed in Room 2.

"Thank you all," I said "It's nice to know what it's finally like to be laid to rest!"

"There you are, nothing that a quick prayer won't solve anytime. Now put the door back as quickly as possible, Mick," said Sister, dashing off to some other duty.

It is not true to say that I did not believe in prayer. On the "good" or "better" days I was in good spirits, full of hopes of going home in the near future. But I firmly believe it was the prayer of others with great faith who brought me through those darkest days, and nights — and were they

31

dark! I had not seen my children for almost two months. My condition and injuries were too unsightly for them to face and I had still not seen a mirror myself.

Friends who tried to comfort me on short visits received little reward for their efforts on some occasions. "I want to *die!*" I would say, "What is there to live for? I shall never have a worthwhile life again. I'm just nuisance value. If you really want to help me give me an overdose of pills!" Sometimes they would be in tears and I would ask selfishly, "What are *you* crying about? *I'm* the one who's suffering."

Many of them afterwards told me that the pub nearest the hospital did a roaring trade during my stay in Steevens' Hospital, as they dashed to it for a large one after "enduring" a visit to me! During this time I recall ironically seeing a Woody Allen film on television. He was walking along in deep depression with, characteristically, hands in his pockets and head down, questioning the Heavens about his sad plight.

"Why *me?*" he asked mournfully, looking up to the sky for an answer. The answer came back from the skies: *"Why not?"* At least it made me smile – and I still use it as a boost the odd time I get depressed now.

It was around this time that I reached an all-time low. I couldn't keep any food down; even hospital foods like Complan or Gevral would nauseate me. My weight went down from my normal seven and a half stone to almost five stone. I had a very high fever and hallucinations from drugs. The pain was never-ending. My thirty-fourth birthday came and went. I didn't care. My husband gave me a beautiful blue negligee set for "when you are better"; I wasn't able to wear it for months. Cards and flowers arrived in armfuls but I hardly asked who they were from.

I became anti-social, refusing visits from even my closest friends. The *nurses* had become my closest friends. I developed kidney infections from the permanent catheter in my urethra. Bedsores were a constant worry but due to the rotary bed and good nursing they rarely became a major problem. My chest became congested from lack of movement, and pleurisy and a pulmonary embolism were another worry, both of which I was to develop later. But the biggest fear at this point was that septicaemia (poisoning of any limb which if it spreads throughout the system is fatal) had set in. Later I realised it was the reason for my total despair. I was as near to death in those few days as I was on two other occasions. Behind the scenes the ever-caring doctors were working to find a drug for my poisoned left leg. It was touch and go.

One Friday night my husband was phoned by the surgeon, Mr B, who was a dear friend. Mr B informed him that amputation of the left leg was almost imperative, but they would have to have his permission first. Distraught, Frank phoned my brother and they arranged to meet at once. They decided they would leave the decision to the doctors who knew best but hoped my life wasn't in danger. It was. Frank asked Mr B what he could do: Should he come in the next day and wait?

"I don't think that would be very good for you," Mr B said. "And Dorine has no idea what is going on and would not be aware of you. Go and play your game of golf as usual and phone me when you get in. There's nothing we can do now but hope."

Frank had arranged to play his Saturday golf with "the lads" at Milltown. Later I asked him what his reaction was.

"I had a sleepless night and went to the golf club early, feeling ghastly. I had several large drinks before the boys arrived and was quite drunk when I went out to the first tee. I couldn't talk about the seriousness of my thoughts."

I thought, how different are the emotional reactions of men and women. A woman under such circumstances would undoubtedly have called her family and closest friends and talked non-stop about the worry and waiting!

That all-important Friday night I had a temperature of 104°/105° and Nurse Ann Murphy from County Wexford was sponging my face gently with cold water around eleven o'clock before she finished her night shift. I felt an extraordinary sense of relief. Everything seemed to slip away as she gently spoke reassuringly to me. Doctors came and went but I didn't hear what they were saying. At around four o'clock in the morning I was more alert and Professor D came into my room. He was a very talented specialist on toxic poisons and infections, septicaemia in particular. One of the biggest problems was that I was still discharging lumps and particles of tarmacadam. Until recently I have had minor operations to remove pieces from my legs.

I recognised the Professor, whom I liked greatly, as he had a lovely gentle manner and always made me smile. I felt better just for seeing him.

"Well, Dorine, sorry to call you so late but I've been working on the poisoned leg all night and we have found the answer! We'll start treating you immediately with the drug and we should have some results around midday."

I could have hugged him – if I had been able to! I suddenly realised the reason for my recent total depression. He explained to me how close I had been to death the previous few days, but he was full of smiles and I started to joke and chat with him – it was the nearest I got to flirting since the fateful night of 23 October!

"Well," he said, as he was leaving, "I'd better get along. My car broke down this morning and I'm using a bike to get around. Also my neighbour had a fire in their house today so we have six visitors to cope with." Off he went smiling goodbye. Such, I thought, is the stuff of which saints are made! That night was in a way another turning point on the road to recovery. I went into a restful sleep feeling almost happy and oddly benumbed by all the caring for the first time in months. I spent two more days in intensive care and then they were confident enough of my condition to return me to my room.

It was a few days before I asked Frank if he knew how bad things had been and he told me of his communication with Mr B and his game of golf.

"How did the golf go?" I asked jokingly.

34

"Appallingly! I hit balls into the woods, bushes, trees, water, everywhere."

"What did you do when you came in?"

"Phoned the hospital and spoke immediately to Mr B who said 'She's going to be okay, and we've saved her leg.' "

"What did you do then?" In typical woman fashion, I was dying to hear of a traumatic display of grief in front of his friends!

"Went back to the lads in the bar and got drunk for the second time in six hours." (He never drinks during the day).

I started to take an interest in what was happening. I even listened to the news the odd time. The nurses read out the letters and cards which continued to arrive daily from caring people. I wanted to see my closest friends again, as I felt I *was* going to make it, even though there was a long, hard road ahead.

Most of all I wanted to see my children, Shane and Tanya. That was arranged for Christmas Day. My husband's secretary, Peggy Scarry, a dear friend of the family, came in to do a Christmas list for me. I wanted to acknowledge some of the care and kindness my family and I had received during those two terrible months. In short, I was beginning to think of *other* people again.

On Christmas morning I was apprehensive and excited as I awaited the children's arrival with Frank. For the first time the nurses tried to improve my dress, but all they could manage was to put a night-jacket around my shoulders. I was still just covered by a sheet. My hands had begun to work slowly again although I could not yet reach my face. I remember having a fear of getting an eyelash in one of my eyes, as I cannot bear anyone touching my eyes. I *still* had not seen a mirror!

Also I was beginning to write again – just my signature. It looked like the writing of a six-year-old, but to me it was a major achievement.

Nurse Roseanne Phelan put a large bandage on my head just before the children arrived.

"Why are you putting that on?' I asked in surprise.

"Well, just so that the children won't see the scar." *I still didn't realise that I had suffered a severely fractured skull.* It suddenly occurred to me that I had not had my hair washed since before the accident. I must have looked a sight! Even my vanity was coming back!

"But my hair! I'll have to have it washed before the children see me. Have we time to do it?'

"Don't worry, they'll be so delighted to see you they won't notice your hair! You look fine," Nurse Phelan assured me. She didn't tell me that the left side of my head was bald. When I was eventually allowed to have my hairdresser, Anita from Peter Mark's in Killiney, come in to start work on what hair I had, it took her eight weeks just to remove all the tarmac, blood and dirt. Just as well I hadn't seen a mirror! And to think I used to worry about getting my hair wet when I was out hunting!

It was heartbreakingly touching to see the children. They were beautifully dressed and obviously under strict instructions to "be quiet" and "not talk too much". All that was forgotten in the excitement of opening the presents I had got for them and it was a relief to distract them as they asked the obvious questions.

"When are you coming home?"

"What happened your head? I thought you only had a broken ankle."

Tanya, aged six, asked: "How do you go to the loo?"

"Oh, I have a tube which Nurse empties into a potty like you used to have!" I explained, laughing.

"Gosh, must be *very* 'barrassing!" said Tanya. "Poor Mum." Shane, who was four years older and looked sweet in his grey suit, was quieter and more vulnerable. Almost shy. But they both looked so happy and healthy that I blessed my dear friend Kathleen Harten, our housekeeper, who looked after them with such care. I felt an even greater determination than ever to get home to them all. Frank was nervous that they would hurt me, as they and I wanted to touch and hug each other. When they left I was filled with mixed emotions of motherly love. I *had* to recover for them. I felt ready to ask the doctors a few straight questions and face up to the full facts. But I felt sure I was going to *win*.

I was still pathetically thin and the doctors were concerned that I was not keeping down any solids. It was suggested that I should try a couple of bottles of Guinness a day, a treatment which turned out to be successful.

Mr P called to see me several times a day and had almost become one of the family, he was so caring. He was a brilliant plastic surgeon who had the major and unenviable task of doing all the skin grafts on my major injuries: almost all my left hip and leg, my right knee, both arms at the elbow, my left wrist and fingers, and almost the whole left side of my head, as well as other "minor" lacerations. Such was the excellence of his work and that of his assistant, Mr D, that not only were all the grafts one hundred per cent successful but the graft to my head, which they feared at the time would need to be repeated in six months, is still very strong and healthy. As a tribute to their work my husband's company, Tedcastle McCormick & Co Ltd, presented to the hospital a special machine which was badly needed in the plastic surgery unit. Happily I have never needed it myself yet, but it has been instrumental in helping Mr P and his colleagues to do extraordinary repair work on serious injuries, including re-attaching severed limbs.

The time had come for me to be transferred to Jervis Street Hospital where the renowned Mr B was head orthopaedic surgeon. Before the accident, he had treated me for minor injuries, from car crashes to hunting falls. He was very handsome, cool and professional and I was rather in awe of him and his "straight from the hip" approach, if you will forgive the double pun (he is one of the countries most accomplished shots in game shooting!)

Although I was to have the same private nurses around the clock I was apprehensive at leaving Steevens', where I had come to feel at home. My room was almost a club, where the nurses would drop in for a chat during break-time. Matron O'Neill was a dear friendly person who gave me constant encouragement. There was also the Floor Sister, a great character from Kerry, who liked nothing better than to have a feed of chocolates when she came on duty at seven o'clock in the morning. Amazingly, she never put on a pound.

But I soon settled into Jervis Street for the next stage of treatment which was, in a way, the most traumatic, as I was now very conscious of everything that was happening to me. All my major orthopaedic surgery was carried out here by Mr B and his team. I still had various recurring infections, mostly affecting the kidneys and the more badly injured limbs. Mr B introduced me to the senior physician, Professor F, whose home city was Cork, just thirteen miles from where I grew up. I was to have many a battle with Professor F whenever I was in one of my "moods" and would refuse certain courses of injections and so on. He was, however, another brilliant Irish doctor who played a major part in saving me on occasions when I was seriously ill again. There were many months ahead before I was to see home despite my own personal "deadline". Unfortunately it wasn't just a question of mind over matter for there was no getting around the healing and rehabilitation processes that my injuries and repair work had to go through.

One of the subjects Professor F had a "thing" about was alcohol, being head of the Liver Unit in Jervis Street. I was still on my Guinness diet of three bottles a day and by sheer coincidence every time he came into the room I seemed to be having one of my bottled meals. One day he asked the nurse to leave us alone for a few moments.

After she had left the room I felt a sense of doom, as I was expecting him to disclose some new complication. To my amazement he said with some hesitation, as if embarrassed:

"Dorine, I don't want to stop anything that helps to ease your pain but I really think if you continue to drink so much you will damage your liver as well as everything else."

For once I was almost speechless. I stammered to explain that it was almost my *full* diet. Eventually the misunderstanding was sorted out. In the following years, however, as the operations dragged on (major ones for at least five years and several minor ones since) I found a large Vodka (leading to four or five every day) or even a bottle of white wine to be a great source of comfort. Hangovers didn't matter as I was in such constant pain anyway. Insomnia became chronic and still is. Every time I change position at night I wake with pain. I visited Prof F with high blood pressure problems in 1979 and told him that I found a few drinks better than any drugs to ease pain and cheer me up. He asked how many I would drink in an average day.

"Well," I said, "I gather doctors always double the amount patients admit to drinking and smoking, but I'll tell you the truth: I drink four or five vodkas every evening or a bottle of wine – and I have no intention of giving it up!"

"Well, if you continue to drink that amount you will be dead in two years," he said very firmly. That was nearly eight years ago and we still laugh when I meet him socially with a glass in my hand!

At home in the early years I needed three large drinks to lessen the pain, before I could get out of bed at midday. Even today, just getting dressed and taking the first steps each day are very painful. On the bad days I look forward to my first drink as an incentive to get up in the evenings.

PART THREE

Illness is the doctor to whom we pay most heed: to kindness, to knowledge we make promises, only pain we obey.

MARCEL PROUST

Doctors . . . know man as thoroughly as if they had made them.

JEAN PAUL SARTRE

In March 1977 I made definite plans to be home for Easter, no matter what my condition or the doctors' opinions. I marked off the days in my diary. I had been moved to St Michael's Private Nursing Home in Dun Laoghaire following a major operation to fuse my right knee. I always went to St Michael's to recover from operations as soon as I was allowed. It was nearer my home and husband's office, and I always felt at home there as I knew all the nurses and staff so well from going there for operations before the accident. Some of my orthopaedic surgery was also carried out in St Michael's. This last operation had involved removing some bone from my right hip and inserting it in my knee to strengthen it so that it could "stabilise" my right leg, which would be able to take my full weight. My left leg was still giving a lot of cause for concern and my surgeon was not sure when it would be able to take any weight. At this time I was still unable to move either of my legs. The operation meant inserting a Steinmann's Pin — a sort of "cross work" of steel into the knee until it had set.

It was not a particularly painful operation and I understood that the pin would be removed within three weeks, when I would be moved back to Jervis Street Hospital to start physiotherapy which would "teach" me to walk again. I presumed the physiotherapy would only take a week or two and was still determined to be home by Easter Sunday on 10 April.

But I encountered other problems which I hadn't allowed for in my plans. Having been on the rotary bed for five months — an ingenious invention created by an Irish doctor, which personally I hated – I had managed to avoid many of the problems which might have developed had I been in an ordinary bed. However, the months of lying in bed without natural movement had taken their toll and I developed a severe pain in my left side. I was so sick of injections that I decided to say nothing in the hope that possibly it was just a pulled muscle. However, within twenty-four hours the pain had become unbearable and on the Saturday night I was hardly able to speak or breathe. My senior physician, Professor F, was called urgently. He told me that I had a "touch" of pleurisy. However, I feared it was something more serious when the entire staff of nurses on the floor seemed to be gathered in my room, among them my private nurse, Margaret Hogan, who is now one of my closest friends. (She lives just a mile away and has saved me in many a crisis.) A specialist in inserting venous drips was called – all my veins had virtually collapsed at this stage – and some time afterwards my physician told me he didn't think it was worth walking the length of the corridor to make the phone call to the "vein expert" that Saturday night as I had, in fact, developed a serious pulmonary embolism.

It was one of the most painful nights of all I had been through that I can recall. There was no time for pain-killers and the only vein that could be used for the anti-coagulant drip which had to be set up to break down the clot was the jugular vein in my neck. Professor F had to hold me down by my shoulders as I screamed in pain. They were all extraordinarily patient and kind and it was a tense night for everyone. My blood pressure had fallen to almost zero. At one stage one of the doctors asked me gently, "Dorine, are you afraid of dying?"

"No," I replied weakly, "just now I'm afraid of living!"

There was an added problem. My left hip was still very badly injured and covered in skin grafts. There was a danger that the anti-coagulant drip could cause a haemorrhage in the hip. *It did.* At this stage I had reached a very low point, physically and mentally. I was so ill I couldn't even feel strong enough to will myself to die. But all the efforts of the doctors and nurses and their constant encouragement were not in vain (no pun intended!).

A week later I was out of danger and picking up strength again. I was told that soon I would be moved to Jervis Street to start physical rehabilitation. I looked forward to having the Steinmann's Pin removed and starting to use my legs again.

It was not long before I was dealt another cruel blow. I presumed the pin was to be left in my right leg for only three weeks.

I remarked to Mr B, "Well, all going well I should be home shortly after Easter." He replied: "But you can't go home with the pin in your leg, and after it comes out you will need intensive physiotherapy."

"But won't the pin be out in three weeks?"

"Three *months*," he said, and all my hopes were dashed.

Once again I was shattered. The great home-coming dream was postponed for what seemed like the hundreth time. Depression set in again. Every time I felt I had overcome a crisis, something even worse seemed to happen.

Only my husband's caring concern and the children kept me going at those times. The children's visits were very important. Their affection and innocent humour were a source of pleasure.

Tanya rushed in one day shouting with delight, "Mummy, my teacher and the class were thrilled today when I told them their prayers were answered!" She had told me frequently that her teacher and the class prayed for me every day. I thought perhaps some miracle had occurred of which I was unaware and I attempted to move my legs hoping for some movement. No luck.

"Well, darling," I asked, "what's the secret miracle?"

"I told them all that yesterday you had your first bath in eight months. They were *thrilled*!" she explained with high delight. I pretended to share her joy although I would have hardly have called the bath a miracle (except that the *nurses* survived the ordeal).

I was carried to the bathroom by three nurses, a feat which inspired me with absolute terror. I was sure they would let me fall, drown, or I would break a leg again. My language during the whole procedure would have been sufficient to frighten a crowd of angry dockers. When I was finally returned to the relative comfort of my rotary bed one of the nurses asked brightly, "Well, now, Dorine, didn't you really enjoy that?"

"*Enjoy* it? Compared to that ordeal, the trip on the towbar was a *treat!*" I replied nastily.

My son Shane behaved in a manner far beyond his ten years. He was fiercely protective of me but obviously deep down extremely anxious to have me home. He always questioned my progress and like myself was always looking for dates for my home-coming and when we could go riding again. Both children had to suffer constant questioning and even teasing at school, as their classmates would hear their parents discussing me at home. As usual in such cases, people often exaggerated. Shane was told by one boy at school that he heard his parents say that both of my legs had been cut off. On another occasion he beat up a boy who had said, "My mum said your mother has no legs! She'll always be in bed as long as she lives."

At that time, knowing I had yet at least another three months before going home, I was again very depressed. Apart from my husband and children and close family I refused to see anyone but Dolores, Pat, Mo, Irene, Brenda and Louise. They were so used to helping me through the various crises and periods of depression that I didn't have to put on an act for them. I could cry, complain or even stay silent. They seemed to understand my various moods. Sometimes I think it's not just a miracle that I survived, but that we *all* survived! It was not until afterwards that I realised the worry and misery *they* went through on my behalf.

The only other people I consented to see were lifelong childhood friends from Cork who often travelled up specially for the day to be told they were just allowed "ten minutes" with me. Many of these reunions were very emotional. These friends knew me only as a very healthy and active person and I suppose I would have been considered wild in my young days, having grown up in a family of five brothers and one sister. In those days it was not unknown for me to arrive into friends' houses around half past seven in the morning waking everyone up and wondering why they were sleeping so late!

In the hospital very early one morning at around half past eight Nurse Phelan answered a knock on the door and came over to me and said, ''There's a friend here to visit you. Would you like to see him?''

''For God's sake, what sort of a clown is he who would expect me to want a visitor at this hour?'' I asked angrily. Back came the inimitable Cork voice of Charlie Hennessy (one of my closest friends) from the door saying, ''I suppose I'm the same sort of clown I always was!'' And of course I had to let him in. Charlie is, incidentally, one of the most versatile and talented people I have ever met. He is a highly successful lawyer and a brilliant conversationalist and comedian. His talented wife, Abbey, is also one of my closest Cork friends but she, like one or two others, couldn't face the experience of seeing me in my ''hospital'' condition. I cried when I saw Charlie but when he left me, I was, as usual, laughing!

''I'm sorry,'' I said through the tears, feeling very self-conscious at that hour of the morning, ''I'm afraid I'm not in very good form today, and I don't look my best.'' He looked at me as if he expected a remark of slightly higher intelligence and said characteristically, ''In the name of Jaysus how could you be in *good form* or looking *your best* after what you've been through?'' Then after a pause while I sniffed away, he said in that resonant voice which no one, even on the Cork stage (where he has often performed), could imitate: ''I think you look lovely!''

I think it was the only time anyone made me laugh at that hour of the morning!

Another Cork visit which I remember was also one of the most traumatic. It was when my childhood friend, Clodagh O'Meara, came to see me. We had experienced all our teenage years together and the happiness and heartache of those times often result in lifelong friendships. She had been one of the head nurses in the Bons Secours Hospital in Cork whenever I was a patient there after the odd car crash or hunting fall. But never was she more important to me than during the traumatic days when our first son was unexpectedly stillborn, although I had been ill all during the pregnancy. I was only twenty-one and hardly married a year. So many memories came flooding back when she visited me this time that we both still wonder if it did either of us any good!

On occasions too, Frank would be at a low ebb himself. The daily hospital visits (sometimes two or three times a day) were depressing and at times after operations very trying for him. For someone who can't bear the sight of a needle it must have been torture to see me with two intravenous drips and a blood transfusion all at the same time.

Everywhere he went, well-meaning people would enquire about my condition. There were always different rumours on the go. At one stage he said he was so upset at having to spend every social outing discussing me with everyone he met that he felt like putting a note on the lapel of his coat with the latest "bulletin" of my condition!

I found I was more at ease with the hospital staff, partly, I supposed, because they had never known me any other way (except in St Michael's). When people who were not among my closest friends visited me I felt embarrassed at their reaction to my injuries. Some left when they saw my legs, and if I couldn't face certain people, they were told that I wasn't allowed any visitors. Nurse Teresa Carey was like a bodyguard at such times. She was also responsible for saving my life on a number of occasions by her excellent nursing and quickness to notice "warning" signals in my condition. She was one of my private nurses from Mrs Shanahan's Agency. Mrs Shanahan and I had become "telephone pals".

Whenever one of my nurses had to leave for a permanent job or to do a course in a different hospital I always phoned Mrs Shanahan myself with the request: "Please send me young cheery nurses, no bossy older ones!" Teresa Carey came to me first in January 1977. At that time I was very upset that Roseanne Phelan was leaving for a permanent job in a Galway hospital. On Teresa's first morning I asked her if she was just staying for the day or the whole week. She looked rather surprised and wanted to know the reason for my question.

"Oh, I was just wondering. I'll be going home in about a week!" I said, full of optimism. As it turned out Teresa stayed with me for a year and a half, living at my home when I was allowed home for short periods between operations in the first two years. Everyone loved her, particularly the children, which was very important to me. She was wonderful at coping with them on my worst days at home when I couldn't bear to let them see me in a state of severe depression or pain.

During my recuperation from the major fusion operations on my right knee in St Michael's Hospital I was particularly depressed at the thought of having a "straight" leg. I had always rather vainly been proud that my legs were one of my best features. Even today nobody but my family and closest friends have seen the injuries on my legs and, to be honest, I still don't much like looking at them myself.

In the early days I felt little consolation when people remarked that I was very lucky to have my legs at all. My orthopaedic surgeon, Mr B, told me some time ago that my case had taken two years off his life. "*Ten* years would be more like it!" quipped his wife.

During that dispiriting time in St Michael's I wouldn't even allow the curtains to be pulled back on my bad days. The sight of healthy, happy people sailing in Dun Laoghaire harbour – the view from my window – made me even more despondent and I felt like screaming when anyone remarked, "Isn't it a lovely day?" I never thought I would experience a "lovely day" again. One of my favourite staff nurses in St Michael's was Marie Byrne. She was particularly good with me when I was deeply depressed and dreaded the days when I wouldn't talk at all. Once she became totally frustrated at my moody silence and in desperation said to me, "Say *anything*, even a four-letter word, but *talk* to us!" At that moment I had a violent spasm of pain in my left foot and obliged with a most unladylike expression which made us all laugh. "Thank God," Marie said, "Anything is better than the silence!" It was psychology such as that which kept me going on many occasions.

I was moved again to Jervis Street Hospital at the end of April 1977 for the physiotherapy treatment to start to move my legs. The head physiotherapist was a delightful person called (ironically) Gerry Walker. I hated physiotherapy, having had some treatment when my hands and arms were beginning to move after some months, and I presumed all physiotherapists were sadistic bullies. Since then I have discovered they are among the kindest people on earth and their difficult job is made more difficult by uncooperative patients.

Since I expected to be out standing on the floor at the end of the first session, it was quite distressing to discover that I could hardly lift my left leg more than an inch off the bed. My right leg seemed to weigh a ton with the Steinmann's Pin and was even more difficult to lift.

However, Gerry Walker and her assistant were full of humour and patience while my moods from one day to the next varied from sheer frustration and bad temper to exhilaration when I began to achieve some small success. One day Mr B came in during my physiotherapy session and a discussion arose about getting me a wheelchair. *A wheelchair!* I was horrified. Wheelchairs were for *invalids* - for people who couldn't walk! I was merely recovering from an accident! I told them there would be no need for one: it would be a waste of money since I would be walking on my own in a couple of weeks.

Gently I was told that I had months of physiotherapy and further operations ahead before I would have any physical independence. It was a shattering revelation. Was there any end to it?

There followed more days of depression and coming to terms with another stage of the trauma since October. Meanwhile the wheelchair was bought. "Isn't it lovely?" some unfortunate nurse said when it arrived. "It's the nicest one I've seen."

"What in the name of God could be nice about a *wheelchair*?" I asked petulantly. I reluctantly agreed to give it a try. The physiotherapy treatment involved being brought to the gym every day by wheelchair. This meant being wheeled down the corridor and lifted down four or five steps (which was terrifying) and then wheeled across a courtyard to the gym where Gerry taught me exercises (from the wheelchair) to strengthen my arms with wall equipment so that I could use the wheelchair independently. I dreaded these sessions even though I received nothing but kindness and encouragement. I resented any of my friends seeing me in the wheelchair and only saw them "by appointment" when I knew I would be back in my bedroom!

The wheelchair experience reached an all-time low one day in early June when the sun was shining and everyone was in a sunny summer mood. My private nurse, Teresa, suggested that maybe I would like an outing in the wheelchair to the park across the road from the Nursing Home in Jervis Street for a bit of sun and fresh air. I agreed, thinking that the sun might have a cheering effect on me. We had no car-rug but I said I wouldn't mind using a blanket instead. I was becoming accustomed to frightening experiences so I made a brave effort to keep calm while I was lifted down the steps of the Nursing Home onto Jervis Street where we had to wait for the traffic lights to turn red to keep the terrifying traffic at bay. It was eight months since I had been in a street.

We arrived safely in the park, which was quite crowded.

Many young people were lying on the grass and elderly people were sitting on benches soaking up the sun. My initial reaction was pleasure at the sun and fresh air. My second reaction was slight embarrassment at being in a wheelchair as I noticed people looking at me and commenting, "The poor thing, she must be an invalid from Jervis Street."

"It must be terrible to be all wrapped up on a hot day like this." I was wearing a dressing gown over my nightie as well as the blanket.

The next reaction was what I afterwards called my "Pied Piper" experience in the park. A few small children started to follow me out of curiosity. Soon more children joined them as well as a few dogs who followed the children. I tried to be patient and dismiss their interest as childish inquisitiveness. But as the crowd of little ones increased their curiosity led them to pester me with questions.

"Did you crash a car, missus?"

"Why have you got a blanket on in the sun?"

"Why are you wearing your night clothes?"

"Have ya no dress?"

"Wha' happened ya?"

After holding my temper for one round of the park with the crowd of children increasing in numbers and interest, I eventually felt I had had enough. Teresa, my nurse, realising my mood and reaction, asked in a rather forlorn way, "Dorine, would you like to stay here another while?"

Before I had time to answer another child shouted: "Have ya no legs, missus?"

It was the final straw. To the horror of my nurse and all nearby I turned around in the wheelchair and shouted at them, "Yes! I have *three* legs, now get lost you horrid little brats!" The children scattered in every direction.

It was the first and last time I visited the park.

The physiotherapy continued and we were making great progress. The physiotherapists and nurses never ceased encouraging me and I feel Mrs Walker deserves a medal for her humour and endurance. A major occasion for the staff and my family and friends was the day I was moved from the rotary bed to a normal hospital bed in my room. The joy of it reminded me of the first time as a child I was changed to a bed from a cot! We all celebrated the occasion.

Finally, the Big Day arrived. I had been fitted with a full-length calliper (a piece of orthopaedic equipment which supports the leg) and was about to attempt my "first steps".

I insisted on dressing in "everyday" clothes for the occasion – the first time I had put on a blouse and skirt since my accident – and going through the ritual *before* I got out of the bed of making up my face and having my hair washed (it still hadn't fully grown on the left side). I was so excited at the thought of just standing upright again that I was nearly too jittery to make the required effort. Slowly and very carefully two physiotherapists and two nurses helped me out of the bed. Speechless with nerves, I slowly straighened up. Then when I felt steady enough with a physiotherapist and a nurse on either side I took my first faltering steps. It was one of the most emotional moments of my life. We walked to the bedroom door and the physiotherapist asked if I would like to take a few steps outside the room.

"Why not?" I asked jubilantly. And when they opened the door all the nurses from the floor were waiting outside to give me a cheer! One of them said "Dorine, this is what makes nursing really worthwhile!" I smiled at her and noticed that she and a few other nurses had tears in their eyes. I started to cry myself, with gratitude, emotion and happiness. I often look back on those few minutes and think with great appreciation of the nursing profession.

The most important thing on that memorable day was once again to make plans for going home. I reckoned a week or two, but once again I was being over-optimistic. The pin still had to be removed from my right leg. After that the leg would be put in full plaster. The left leg was very weak and I had to wear the calliper every time I got out of bed. I was progressing to walking with a walking aid, and was still only taking very shaky steps but I was *walking*!

I could think of nothing else but going home even though I still had major injuries to cope with. My arms were still weak and there were more operations on my left leg to face. Tarmac was still causing infection in all sorts of places (and often had to be removed under anaesthetic for several years afterwards). I bullied, cajoled, appealed and tormented my doctors to allow me home. We finally came to a compromise. Mr B gave his consent, provided I had around the clock nurses, the wheelchair, a walking aid, and of course my left leg in the calliper and my right leg in full plaster. The date was set for 7 July – I was to return on 12 September for more major surgery, but for the moment all my thoughts were centred on the fact that I was GOING HOME!

PART FOUR

Once I laughed at the power of love,
And twice at the grip of the grave
And twice I patted my God on the head
That man might call me brave!

RUDYARD KIPLING

The joy of meeting pays the pangs of absence;
else who could bear it?

ANON

The seventh of July 1977 was one of the most emotional days of my life. Three of my closest friends, Brenda, Pat and Dolores, came to see me off from the hospital, as well as the entire nursing staff from my floor and Teresa, my private nurse, who was coming home to stay with me. It was a major performance to transfer me from the wheelchair to the car seat. But at least it wasn't an ambulance. I hardly spoke on the way home, just watched everything along the way and thought of how long I had waited for this day.

I deliberately asked my husband to let a driver collect me and misinformed him of the time of arrival at home so that he would miss the emotional first minutes which I knew would be too traumatic for both of us. As we drove through the avenue gates I thought I had never seen any place look so lovely. The garden was a blaze of colour, thanks to Bertie, our gardener, with the lawns almost manicured and my beloved trees surrounding the house greener than ever.

We pulled up at the front door. Shane, Tanya, and Kathleen, our housekeeper, to whom I owed so much, rushed out to meet me. It was a joyful reunion. I had to use the wheelchair, of course, and dear Teresa's help but I was *home*.

I headed straight for the drawing room. Brenda, Dolores and Pat were with me and when I was wheeled into the drawing room I was speechless at the welcome which awaited me. The room was like the Chelsea flower show, there were so many bouquets and arrangements of flowers. There were fifty or sixty "welcome home" cards and telegrams and even champagne on ice! The children were ecstatic and we all hugged each other in celebration. I was about to open the first telegram when the phone rang and I said, "That's hardly for me!"

One of my friends answered it.

"It's for you, alright," she laughed. "A very special person."

It was no less important a person than Jack Lynch, the then Taoiseach (and a close friend) to welcome me home. One of Jack's greatest charms is his personal touch but never did it matter more than at that moment. I had barely put the phone down when it rang again.

"Welcome home, darling," said Frank. He had been phoning every ten minutes for two hours before!

"You're late," I said, "The Taoiseach made it before you!"

The children presented me with "welcome home" poems and gifts and their own little flower arrangements. Probably the most touching item was a big colour poster painted by Shane, on which he had written: "Welcome Home Mum. It has been 296 days without you. 296 sad long lonely days without you. All my love, Shane." It said it all. It was worth all the pain, all the depression, all the fight for survival to be back in the only place I wanted to be in the world.

The next few weeks was a period of adjustment, full of excitement and happiness. The constant pain which I suffered from my left leg and an infection under the plaster on the right leg couldn't take away from the dream come true. Although I still had to have live-in nurses they were completely kind and sensitive to my situation and they soon became part of the family. Kathleen, my housekeeper, was almost as emotional as I was at the home-coming. Shane remarked of her: "She was a mother and father to us, Mum." Sadly, her own health was under stress for some time and she had to retire from our household to rest for six months on doctor's orders. Unfortunately, she was unable to return to us after that time. We have never lost touch with her since and the children constantly visit her.

One of the first things I did in those early days at home was to go back to the Willow Grove and retrace my horrific journey up the lane ten months earlier. It was something I had to do and it proved to be a valuable therapeutic exercise.

The next major milestone occurred one day when I asked one of the nurses to help me into the driver's seat of my own car, the automatic Triumph Stag.

"You're not thinking of driving, are you?" she asked with some consternation.

"Oh no, I just want to get the feel of it," I said. She sat in beside me and I turned on the ignition. Immediately I felt totally at ease and began to put it into gear. Then to the astonishment of everyone looking on I found myself driving down the avenue while the brave nurse encouraged me but cautioned me to "take it easy!" In this mood of exhilaration I went for a ten-mile drive around the County Wicklow roads and returned with a wonderful sense of achievement. One of the great pleasures left to me now is to be able to get into the car and drive anywhere I want and be totally alone.

Due to my limited mobility I feel a real frustration in my dependence on others (as I walk on two sticks), but driving on my own is one of the few pleasures I can enjoy with complete independence. It is also the only time I enjoy being in a car. As a passenger every jolt or bump on the road is very painful to my legs and back, but when I am driving myself I don't notice them.

On 12 September I was booked into Jervis Street again for a major operation which left my leg half an inch shorter than the right one. I was in hospital again for my thirty-fifth birthday but was allowed home for Christmas. I was determined to get back to running the house and being as supportive as possible to Shane and Tanya. I wanted to fulfil my role as mother and wife to the best of my ability.

We had a wonderful new housekeeper, Chrissie Branigan, who came to us after Kathleen left. She found our house rather too far from her home in Ballymun and was considering leaving as soon as I found someone else. She didn't realise how distressed I was about trying to make arrangements for the children, before returning to hospital for three months until a friend told her of my impending hospitalisation. She came to my bedroom and finding me in floods of tears, she held my hand and said: "Don't worry, madam, I didn't realise you were going in for a big operation. I wouldn't dream of letting you down so I'll stay till you are home and well again." I was so relieved and touched by the kindness of a relative stranger.

Well, she stayed with us for ten years and her devotion and caring couldn't be surpassed. She only left in the spring of 1987, aged seventy years. One of her great gifts apart from her excellence in housekeeping was being sensitive to my moods on the bad days. She comes from the famous garda "Lugs" Branigan family. The late lamented "Lugs" sadly didn't live up to the family tradition of longevity: he died last year aged seventy-two. Only last year Chrissie went to Tipperary (her home county) for the funeral of her uncle Paddy who was aged a hundred and three when he died!

When I came out of hospital that Christmas I was in a wheelchair again and the first social outing I managed to work up the nerve to face was a party at the home of close friends. The experience was quite traumatic: some people were nervous of meeting me, others queued up to say "Hello" and "Welcome back". My hosts were very sensitive to my situation.

I have been touched by the extraordinary kindness of people at unexpected times and could not write this book without mentioning the understanding, sensitivity and affection (even on my most bad-tempered days) of my friends Dolores Lynch, Pat Rowan and Louise Keegan.

Coming home from hospital marked the start of the long road back to leading as normal a life as possible. Of course my life has changed totally since that night ten years ago. While I could never again have the sporting life I enjoyed, what was more distressing was the fact that I could no longer participate in any of my children's sporting activitites. Even now when I watch them from the window going for a walk through the fields with their father, my eyes fill up with sadness because I cannot be with them.

The other things I miss most are really the simplest things in life. I cannot walk barefoot, go for a walk through the fields or on a beach, either on my own or with my family. My dependence on other people is also very frustrating as I was an extremely independent person before the accident. My personality hasn't changed, so it is often difficult to come to terms with my dependence and I face a psychological battle daily. Little things affect me greatly like not being able to send off a letter privately because someone else has to post it! Even though I only sleep for about half an hour at a time at night, when I wake from my "last sleep" of the night for a few seconds I *still* think the accident was a nightmare until I start to move and the pain very quickly brings me back to the reality. And the sheer *horror* of that mile-long journey on the towbar of the horsebox is rarely out of my thoughts for more than a few minutes.

Now, however, I can look back with some pride at how well the children survived the whole ordeal of seeing me mostly in pain and suffering during their formative years. They are enormously helpful – and uncomplaining on my bad days – and seem to have developed, as a result of their experience, a great feeling of caring for people. Also happily they have been normal teenagers, breaking into tantrums and making demands, making me feel like any normal mother of teenagers with all the frustrations *that* involves!

On the days when I was depressed I used to feel I had to protect them from seeing me in tears and lying in bed with the curtains still drawn. At such times I would perhaps not have even a cup of tea all day and I used to ask my housekeeper to say I was asleep. Then I gradually realised how much this behaviour upset them as they wanted to share my sadness or frustration. So now they come in and hold my hand and chat about everything, which helps us all.

Often people ask if I have ever thought of suicide. I most certainly have! Maybe it would be truer to say that sometimes I wish I hadn't lived. Of course there are times when I feel that the pain and frustration and limitations of my lifestyle are very hard to cope with. But so far I have always said, in the darkest hours, usually lying awake in pain at night alone, or facing another operation: "I feel like giving up *now*, but I'll wait till tomorrow." And the next day I always find there is a reason for living. One of my family or friends phones or calls by with a problem, I get a special letter in the post or someone wants to see me about something and I am the only one who can help – and so I keep going.

Talking of suicide, an amusing incident comes to mind. One day a couple of years ago a close friend who was having a lot of personal problems came to see me unexpectedly. I told her I was too depressed to chat but she said, "I'm very depressed too and I want to talk about *my* problems, but I won't stay long.'

"All right," I said grumpily, selfishly thinking only of my own predicament.

We discussed her problems and tried to sort them out.

"Have you ever thought of suicide?" she asked.

"Of course," I replied, "but I have the perfect plan. I've thought of every aspect of it. I could drown in our pool, which would look like an accident, but apparently people look awful if they die from drowning and I want to look a nice corpse."

"Then I could take an overdose of pills, but knowing my luck I wouldn't even go to sleep, and would probably end up with a stomach pump which I couldn't bear. And also everyone would know I had tried to commit suicide."

I thought at this stage my friend would be *distraught* at the idea of me taking my own life after all I had been through, but to my surprise – and annoyance – she seemed calmly interested.

"Well?" she said.

"Well," I continued," I could throw myself off the

balcony but I would probably just break a leg again." I paused for dramatic effect.

"So what would your final solution be?"

"The gun, can't go wrong. Oldest trick in the book. Always looks like an accident. I would call out that I heard a burglar in the house and then when everyone is running around looking for the burglar I would shoot myself through the heart: totally simple and no nasty gossip!"

I expected her to show deep grief and emotion at the very thought of my plan but after a few moments she said: "Do you know something? I think that's an *excellent* idea."

I was so taken aback by her nonchalance that any ideas of suicide I have ever entertained since I have kept strictly to myself!

PART FIVE

If you confer a benefit, never remember it; if you receive one, never forget it.

CHILON

In faith and hope the world will disagree,
But all mankind's concern is charity.

ALEXANDER POPE

It is now ten years since that fateful day in October 1976 and so much has happened in the meantime. Our children have grown up. Our son Shane, aged twenty-one, is at college in Pittsburgh University, Pennsylvania: our daughter Tanya, aged seventeen, is in boarding school in England and will be doing her "A" level exams in 1988. So in a sense I have completed my role in rearing my children – if a mother ever does complete that job! Sometimes I feel that my husband could do without me, when I am in one of my "nuisance value only" moods!

Also as I said earlier, at times when I feel I am no use to them anymore I usually find that the next day one of them comes to me with some problem which I am able to sort out or have to organise. I am certain that no matter what I am going through, my family is worth every sleepless night and every twinge of pain.

One of the great aids in my recovery has been the sense of humour I have shared with my family and friends. For instance, we always laugh if anyone uses such an expression as "Give me a break!" or "That's a bit near the bone!"

We say "Sorry, that's not allowed in our house!"

I absolutely refuse to allow anyone to refer to me as an "invalid" or "handicapped" or "disabled". Of course I am disabled to some extent, but if I had accepted that label from the start I would probably have settled for a wheelchair and not made the huge effort to walk again.

When people refer to my condition I merely say, "I am recovering from a serious accident" or "I just happen to walk more slowly than other people." Teddy Kennedy Junior, who had a leg amputation when he was aged ten, was quoted recently in the papers as saying: "I never consider myself an invalid, I consider myself 'physically challenged' ". I find this a most inspiring definition.

My ambition is to be once again as athletic as he is, and I never lose the dream of horse-riding again. Meanwhile I would be happy just to be able to do very mundane things such as the weekly shopping, go for a walk in the fields or on a beach or cook a simple meal.

My life today ten years later is a very mixed experience. There are some wonderful days and pleasurable evenings but these alternate with days of ghastly pain, dreadful depression, frightening operations or one of my "conditions" acting up. I have always been helped to the point of being spoilt by my wonderful family, friends, doctors and nurses.

As a small tribute to paying back something of my life which I owe to the Irish medical profession I have agreed on a number of occasions to join hospital boards or fund-raising committees. I have tried to respond to all of these requests (starting in 1983) but for a number of reasons I put my major effort into fund-raising for St Vincent's Hospital Research and Development Fund. I am not, by nature, a "committee" person but I was strongly encouraged by the then chairman of the Board of Trustees, Margaret Heffernan, and I agreed to have a go. Two years earlier I had been approached by St Michael's Hospital in Dun Laoghaire to raise funds. I agreed as long as I did not have to be a member of a committee (I didn't agree with some of the policies of some board members). I said I would try to raise funds privately as that is my best way of working.

I sent out seventy personal letters asking each company or individual to contribute one hundred pounds toward fund-raising for St Michael's. To my amazement, within two weeks I received no less than *sixty-seven* cheques for one hundred pounds each.

We had a small reception at St Michael's at which I handed over the money and there was a small draw of three or four prizes for the contributors. I was then toasted with champagne. To my delight and amusement some of the oldest members of the community – in their eighties – shared in the "bubbly"!

St Vincent's fundraising was a more ambitious undertaking. And at times it became overwhelming due to my painful condition and insomnia.

For a start, their target, set by the Board of Trustees of which I became a member, was three million pounds for the Research and Development Fund. It was indeed a daunting task but Margaret Heffernan is not easily daunted when it comes to a challenge. As I said, since I was not a committee person at heart, I thought I would do better on my own. I decided to think out some scheme whereby I could work from home on the basis of my own ideas.

As I lay awake at night I thought about what I had done for St Michael's, and wondered if the same idea would work again. I knew asking for a hundred pounds would be a long, drawn-out task, since I aimed to raise a hundred thousand pounds, so I decided I would have to "aim high" and ask people or companies for at least *one thousand pounds* each. I organised a lunch in my home with Margaret Heffernan and John Duffy (Development Director, St Vincent's Hospital Research and Development Fund) to discuss the matter. I had made a list of the people and companies I would approach.

Margaret and John were somewhat sceptical of my chances of success. Many of the people on the list had been approached before or had already contributed to St Vincent's. I was not put off by this attitude even when people said I would be lucky to raise ten thousand pounds. I knew all I needed was an emotive catch-line so I spent some time considering the wording of my "begging letter", which would be all-important. Margaret and John eventually left the house, wishing me every success and support. I think they thought I was a bit mad.

I was *determined* to prove I could do it and lay awake for nights trying to find the right formula. I knew my personal story would have some appeal but I needed just a little more.

I was staying in Ashford Castle in County Mayo one Friday night in July. My husband was abroad and I had travelled to County Mayo with some friends for the wedding of one of my favourite nurses, Veronica Flannery, who was marrying Stephen Tarpey the following day.

As usual I was lying awake in the middle of the night for several hours. I had been told by the hotel staff that I was in the Ronald Reagan suite and since, presumably, I was sleeping in his bed, I did a "Reagan" and suddenly out of the blue thought of a wonderful idea to use in my "begging" letter.

I would explain to people in the letter that I had been through a dreadful accident and that if they only *knew* what Irish medicine had done to save my life they would all send blank cheques for St Vincent's Hospital to me at once. I dashed to the writing desk to put this down on paper, but by now it was 5 am and I realised I was very hungry. I rarely eat during the day but I am often starving when I lie awake at night. I remembered with dismay that room service did not start till half-past eight. Then I had a flash of brilliance (I must have been sleeping on Nancy Reagan's side of the bed): As an emotive piece of persuasion I decided I would fast one day a week from the day I sent out my letters until I had achieved my target of one hundred thousand pounds.

I couldn't wait to wake up my friends who had travelled with me for the wedding and tell them of my plan. So great was my enthusiasm that at half-past eight on the dot, I phoned room service for my friends Pat and Dolores and ordered their breakfasts as well as my own so that we could have a "board meeting" about my ingenious idea! At this hour of the morning they didn't think it was the best idea I ever had. My friends refused to wake up. As I had ordered the breakfasts from my own room and there were six stairs down to the door from the Reagan bed I couldn't manage to get down on my sticks to open the door. Consequently I ended up at the start of my "fast" with *three* cooked breakfasts outside my door on the floor.

A County Mayo waiter later said to me with no animosity, "Don't worry, some very odd people have stayed here, sure we even had the Reagans!"

Finally we all had a later breakfast at which I conducted the " board meeting" with my friends before we left for the wedding in the beautiful Ballintubber Abbey. Incidentally, the wedding was a huge success and I ate everything in sight, keeping in mind the weekly fast ahead.

"You're mad, quite mad, you can't go without food for a whole day," Dolores said, tucking into her hearty Irish breakfast Ashford-style.

"What will the doctors say?" asked Pat. "I thought they were supposed to be worried about your health?"

"I'm making the money for some of them," I said, adding, "if I do make any."

"It's blackmail — Everyone knows what suffering you've been through and they will feel they *have* to pay up."

"I know," I said, "that's why I think it's a good idea."

A week later I sent out the letters, as follows:

August 1985

Dear _____

I hope you are enjoying a pleasant healthy breakfast on this grand soft summer morning!

I also wish you a happy, healthy day, whether you are on your way to a board meeting, a race meeting, a holiday, a shopping spree, a lunch appointment or whatever your day's business may be. Isn't it good to know that you can plan without any worries about your health, your independence in your work, or your privacy, should you wish to be alone?

(I have read your horoscope for today and it says "This morning you will receive an unexpected letter and you will write a cheque for a cause which will give you great

71

satisfaction. £1,000, £2,000, £3,000 perhaps?'')

But what, you may ask, can you get today for a thousand pounds that is money well spent and gives pleasure and satisfaction?

A gold watch?
A colour T V ?
A camera?
1000 pints of Guinness?
A weekend in London?
2 designer suits?
A crocodile handbag?
A work of art?

But you probably have all of these things already!

There is another way to spend £1,000 which will not only give you satisfaction but will give hope and health to possibly thousands of Irish people who not only suffer poor health but have never dreamed of owning a car, or a stereo, or a camera or having a holiday abroad.

I have been critically ill and close to death on a number of occasions following a serious accident nine years ago. Since then, I have had over fifty operations and due to the medical skill and dedication of Irish doctors and nurses, I am now once again leading a very full life, even if some of my activities are limited.

It was not only the expertise and efficiency of the staff in many hospitals which impressed me (which saved my life and limbs) but on many occasions it was the caring and concern which ''kept me going'' far beyond the call of medical duty.

Money does not pay for this sort of human dedication. But money is necessary to train the nurses and doctors, to pay for medical research and the upkeep of the hospital facilities and vital equipment.

St Vincent's hospital is one of the main training hospitals in Ireland. Its name is synonymous world-wide with medical excellence and efficiency.

Many people say "I hate hospitals". After fifty-two operations you may think I, too, would say that. On the contrary, I am fully aware of other people's fears and sufferings in hospitals and equally aware of the dedicated work done twenty-four hours a day in Irish hospitals. Consequently, I feel committed to helping hospital projects in any way I can. I am glad to have the opportunity to show people who are fortunate enough never to have experienced serious illness how much they can help.

St Vincent's Hospital frequently holds seminars attended by General Practitioners from all over Ireland. These seminars are of great importance in allowing doctors in their local work to benefit from the knowledge, expertise and world-wide experience of the best consultants in St Vincent's.

The Fundraising Campaign is to provide the necessary facilities for this work to be carried out in a fully equipped centre from which every aspect of Irish medical work will benefit the whole community.

So far, Irish companies and individuals have contributed £1.5 million to St Vincent's. Our target is £2.5 million. It is my personal target to raise £100,000 by December (Well, look at what Bob Geldof did!).

To show my personal dedication to this project, I shall be fasting for one day a week (water only permitted) until my target is reached!

Thank you for reading this letter. I am not only hopeful but quite confident of your immediate generous response.

The names of all those who contribute will be put "in a hat" and the person whose name is drawn first will win £5,000. There will be other prizes of not less than £1,000.

So as you finish your breakfast and I start my first day's fasting, perhaps you will take out your cheque book before you go. Thousands of people will thank you in the future. Maybe one day one of your own family, or even *you* may benefit.

Meanwhile, I wish you and your family a happy and healthy day – every day!

Please send your donations payable to:-
St Vincent's Hospital Educational Trust Limited and post to me:

Dorine Reihill

_____

_____

_____

(Do it now - you will feel better)

Yours Sincerely,

_____

Dorine V. Reihill, Trustee.

The response was *extraordinary*. I received everything from hilarious replies (men who *didn't* have crocodile handbags or designer dresses!) to cheques for two or three thousand pounds as well as twenty-thousand-pound four-year convenants. I was totally overwhelmed. Kevin Myers of the *Irish Times* ran a three-day story in his column about my accident, survival and fund-raising efforts and called on everyone to chip in at once, *or else,* and people don't dismiss Kevin Myers lightly, I can tell you.

That seemed to do the trick: Not only were the thousand pound cheques coming in but there were also pound notes and fifty pence postal orders from little old ladies and children. And I felt I had to answer every one of them personally: a task far more demanding than missing my morning tea one

end. But I am confident that with the advances of modern medicine one day in the future I shall once again be *just an ordinary housewife*.

EPILOGUE

A few years ago I was going abroad (travel is a nightmare for me nowadays due to the discomfort, pain, and fear of crowds) and I was advised by one of my surgeons to ask my family doctor to write out a brief list of my medical problems should any emergency arise when I was away. The ''brief'' list consisted of two long typed pages naming all my injuries: broken legs, broken arms, wrist, fingers and vertebrae. Besides my orthopaedic problems there were other items such as asthma, blood pressure, bronchitis, chronic insomnia, diverticulitis, and so on. The list ended with the caution: ''She is allergic to almost everything.''

That list gave me the idea of writing an Alphabetical Index for this book, which would be a summary of what my experiences have been for the past ten years.

September 1987

INDEX A-Z

A

Anaesthetics. I have had approximately sixty operations to date that I can recall, all involving anaesthetics. Some of them involved major surgery and others were for pain-killing injections which I need every few months. My veins have become so "worn out" through the years since the accident that it is very difficult now to find a suitable one when necessary.

Allergies. I am allergic to almost everything, from tobacco smoke to newspaper print. I am constantly breaking out in a scarlet fever-type rash.

B

Blood Pressure. This is a constant problem as I suffer from high blood pressure.

Bronchitis. Another one of my ailments.

Blood Donors. To me, these are the unacknowledged "heroes" of medicine.

C

Caring people. I have been lucky to have had the loving care of many people, in particular my children, Shane and Tanya.

Childhood. A source of happy memories and friendships which still endure.

D
Death. The experience of being so close to death on many occasions has greatly changed my attitude to life.

Doctors. I have boundless admiration for their enormous dedication to their work which is truly a vocation. One surgeon said to me once, "It *is* a vocation; anyone who goes into medicine for the money doesn't last long." Doctors are also notoriously bad patients, as any nurse will tell you! I recall one occasion when one of my surgeons was having a minor hernia operation. He was in a room near mine. One night the nurse came in to give him the customary suppository which he insisted on administering in private himself. A while later he was seen leaving his room to go to the toilet. After some time he emerged and was walking back to his room when a young nurse innocently asked with a cheery smile, "Did everything go alright?" His bad-tempered reply was: "How the hell do I know? The bloody light wasn't working! Get a new bulb in there at once!"

E
Epitaph. I often thought of what my epitaph would be, especially on those occasions when I was dying. I was discussing my injuries with a friend one day when she jokingly asked me what I would like on my gravestone. I told her that after what I had heard from my surgeons in the past week, I had come up with the following:

DORINE V. REIHILL

REST IN PIECES

F
Fear. One of the most overpowering emotions I have experienced. Sometimes, when I am in crowds or at the top of steep steps, I experience sheer terror. On one occasion in Spain, I actually fainted at the top of a marble staircase. Fear

is much harder to cope with than pain and is the source of most of my nightmares.

Friendship. *"Friendship is the only cement that will ever hold the world together."* Woodrow Wilson.

Fund-Raising. Fund-raising for charities has been a very satisfying experience in the past few years. I am delighted to have had the opportunity to pay something back to Irish hospitals.

G
Goodness. All these people whom I was lucky enough to meet during my recovery radiated this quality. In ten years I experienced only two unpleasant incidents concerning people.

Guinness. This kept me alive when I couldn't eat anything else, although on one occasion it got me into trouble with my chief physician, through a misunderstanding!

H
Horror. The sheer horror of what happened on that fateful night never leaves me.

Hope. Fortunately this never left me either, or I would have given up the fight for survival very early on, when I was first aware of my awful injuries.

Horses. These have always been part of my life. As I can no longer hunt (*yet*) I have started to follow racing and have had an interest in racehorses as an owner for some years. I am also fond of the "odd bet." One of the oddest bets I had was in hospital. I was lying awake one night in hospital, very worried about two major operations I was facing the following morning. To take my mind off my worries, I decided to study the racing form in the evening papers and to pick out a few bets for the following day when I came back from theatre.

I eventually picked out four horses, convinced that not another person in Ireland could know as much as I did about the horses running the following day. I decided to do a one pound "Yankee" (£11 investment) on the four horses I picked out.

I came back from the theatre in a daze around lunch-time. I had ordered a morning paper which was on my bed. I suddenly remembered the horses and grabbed the paper for the racing page which I opened. To my annoyance I saw ten of everything, I was still so drugged.

In a haste I searched for the names and numbers of the horses which I had spent four hours studying the night before. I couldn't remember any of them and the more I tried to concentrate the more hazy everything looked. Finally, I gave up the effort and just picked out four jockeys from four races. I phoned a bookmaker who thought I sounded somewhat odd.

"I'm just out of an anaesthetic and three hours in theatre," I explained, and gave him the names of the jockeys and asked him for the names of their horses. I placed my bets and forgot about it until the next morning when the bookie phoned and said, "*Please* don't make any more bets under anaesthetic!" All four horses – outsiders – had won and to my amazement my bet paid a hundred to one! So much for studying form!

I

I am alive! Descartes formulated the phrase, "Cogito ergo sum" ("I think, therefore I am"). At one stage *thinking* was about all I was capable of doing.

Insomnia. I suffer from chronic insomnia and no amount of pills or medication help. I can take enough pills to "kill a cow" and still not close an eye, so I gave them up years ago. I now prefer a few drinks in the evening and if I find sleep impossible I write or read.

Unfortunately I need a lot of sleep and after a sleepless night I am often physically exhausted and have to nap during the day.

J

Jervis Street. The hospital where most of my important orthopaedic surgery was carried out by Mr B. I have many happy memories of rehabilitation there.

K

Ken. This is my beloved and devoted brother, who not only kept my hopes alive but was a tower of strength to my husband.

In the beginning Ken was marvellous at taking charge of the situation while everyone was still suffering from shock and he visited me three times a day. For two weeks the nurses thought he was a doctor, and he was automatically allowed in! I remember one occasion during the first few weeks when I was in and out of a coma and didn't know the day, week or month. Ken asked me was there anything special I would like and I said "Strawberries" (It was mid-November). The next day he came in with a tin of strawberries. I don't recall my reaction but apparently I put on a cross expression, because I wanted *fresh* strawberries. Poor Ken was quite hurt. A few days later he arrived with a punnet of fresh strawberries purchased in London! Unfortunately, I was too ill to eat them.

L

Life. My traumatic experience has convinced me that life is for living. The letter "**L**" also brings to mind an off the cuff remark I once made to Tony O'Reilly. When I arrived walking on two sticks at his home in County Kildare one day, Tony exclaimed, "Dorine, I expected you in a wheelchair or a stretcher!" I told him, in no uncertain terms, that I was not an invalid, but just recovering from an accident. He said: "But how on *earth* did you survive all those injuries and operations?'' I replied somewhat facetiously, "Love, Laughter and Liquor.''

M
Mad. At one stage, I said to a friend, "Isn't it amazing, I didn't go mad, looking back over it all?'' To my surprise she replied, "What makes you think you're not?'' Enough said on that subject.

N
Nights. They seem endless with my insomnia and nightmares.

Nurses. I can't pay them sufficient tribute. I have met some of the finest people in Ireland among this profession and am happy to count nurses among my best friends.

O
Operations. The total number: around sixty to date. In the early weeks I had to go to theatre for an anaesthetic just to change the dressings on my injuries, as if they tried to do it in my room I might have gone into shock.

P
Pain. A constant companion which I have learnt to live with. I must admit, however, that it does not make *me* easier to live with! The only time my legs are without pain is when I am in the heated swimming pool, which gives me great enjoyment; I play music while I am in the pool and can literally dance in the water. Dancing is something I miss greatly.

Q
Queries. My constant query was about when I was GOING HOME. Also the eternal question, "What *good* did it all do?''

R

Religion. It played a changing role in my time in hospital. As I remarked in the book, I think other people's prayers were far more effective than my own! One long-time friend who visited me said a curious thing. He was a well-known non-believer, yet he told me, "Dorine, God must have saved you for something special." And yet he confesses to being a practising atheist!

S

Shane. Our son, a shining example of love and bravery.

T

Tanya. Our daughter, a continuing source of joy.

Teenagers. Happily they are both healthy teenagers with the I-know-it-all attitude and the conflicts which are part of those years. It makes me feel I really have made it as a "normal" mother.

Theatre. On one occasion when the anaesthetist, Dr R, was about to knock me out for an operation I remarked, "Do you know, I always wanted to be an actress but I never thought I would be playing a major role in a *hospital* theatre sixty times!"

U

Unbelievable. This describes the human instinct for survival in the face of the most extraordinary circumstances.

V

Veins. I have had so many anaesthetics, injections, drips, blood transfusions, etc, that my veins have nearly all collapsed, so now it is a problem whenever I need an anaesthetic or a blood test.

W

Wishes. My dearest wish is to wake up and discover it was all just a bad dream. Even after ten years, I wake up after a short sleep at night believing it was a nightmare until the first movement brings instant pain and reality.

X

X-Rays. I have undergone hundreds of them. I spent one afternoon in hospital going through them all and was quite fascinated at the intricacies of the human body, particularly when it is smashed to bits and put together again! I jokingly suggested I should have a few of the more interesting Picasso-like ones framed!

Y

You. This is a vote of thanks for all of you who have helped me through the last ten years. I hope this book will help some of you who may have had other tragic experiences.

Yesterdays. I look back happily on the "good old days" when I enjoyed the good life. However, there is much that gives me pleasure and I am able to participate in many things once again with much fulfilment. And there is always tomorrow . . .

Z

Zest. I still have a great *zest* for life and all my many interests, and hope to continue to do so.